Praise for *Pure Dead Magic*:

'A rollicking good tale . . . enjoyment' *Independent*

'Original, challenging, entertaining and, frankly, bizarre . . . warm and hilarious, highly individual literary style which crackles with energy' *Guardian*

'Absolutely brilliant . . . full of laughter and puns . . . And . . . the best witch character I have ever come across' *Bookseller*

'Gliori . . . reveals a talent for wild comedy, linguistic invention and pastiche. *Pure Dead Magic* features a cellarful of mythical beasts, a nanny who bears a distinct resemblance to Mary Poppins, a talking tarantula and even the Mafia . . . Wonderful stuff' *Daily Telegraph*

'It's a gallimaufry of ghastly giggly stuff . . . good, disgusting fun' *Financial Times*

'Fast-moving, over-the-top, engaging and great fun . . . a jolly good read' *Books for Keeps*

Also available by Debi Gliori
in the *Pure Dead Magic* sequence:

PURE WICKED
PURE DEAD BRILLIANT
DEEP TROUBLE

Pure Dead Magic

by Debi Gliori

CORGI BOOKS

PURE DEAD MAGIC
A CORGI BOOK : 0 552 55367 0

First published in Great Britain by Doubleday
a division of Random House Children's Books

PRINTING HISTORY
Doubleday edition published 2001
Corgi edition published 2002

This Ottakar's special edition published 2005

1 3 5 7 9 10 8 6 4 2

Text and illustrations copyright © Debi Gliori, 2001

The right of Debi Gliori to be identified as the author of this work has
been asserted in accordance with the Copyright Designs and
Patents Act 1988.

Set in 12/15½pt Palatino

Corgi Books are published by Random House Children's Books,
61–63 Uxbridge Road, London W5 5SA,
a division of The Random House Group Ltd,
in Australia by Random House Australia (Pty) Ltd,
20 Alfred Street, Milsons Point, Sydney, NSW 2061, Australia,
and in New Zealand by Random House New Zealand Ltd,
18 Poland Road, Glenfield, Auckland 10, New Zealand
and in South Africa by Random House (Pty) Ltd,
Endulini, 5a Jubilee Road, Parktown 2193, South Africa.

Printed and bound in Great Britain by
Cox & Wyman Ltd, Reading, Berkshire.

For My Family and Other Beasts

With grateful thanks to the Scottish Arts Council
for keeping the wolf from the door
and to the beautiful west coast of Scotland
for providing the inspiration

Contents

Dramatis Personae

THE FAMILY

TITUS STREGA-BORGIA – the twelve-year-old hero
PANDORA STREGA-BORGIA – the ten-year-old heroine
DAMP STREGA-BORGIA – their fourteen-month-old sister
SIGNOR LUCIANO AND SIGNORA BACI STREGA-BORGIA –
parents of the above
STREGA-NONNA – great-great-great-great-great-great-
grandmother (cryogenically preserved) of Titus, Pandora and Damp

THE GOOD HELP THAT WAS HARD TO FIND

MRS FLORA McLACHLAN – nanny to Titus, Pandora and Damp
LATCH – butler
MARIE BAIN – cook

THE BEASTS

MULTITUDINA – rat, mother to multitudes, and Pandora's pet
TARANTELLA – spider with attitude
SAB, FFUP AND KNOT – mythical Schloss dungeon beasts
TOCK – crocodile inhabitant of Schloss moat

THE ITALIAN CONNECTION

DON LUCIFER DI S'EMBOWELLI BORGIA – half-brother of
Luciano Strega-Borgia
DON CHIMERA DI CARNE BORGIA – grandfather (deceased) of
Titus, Pandora and Damp
PRONTO – Don Lucifer's *consigliore* (adviser)

*All resemblance to persons living or dead is unintentional, but the author wishes to
acknowledge a definite similarity between herself and Tarantella.*

from GREAT SCOTTISH HOUSES YOU CAN'T AFFORD
(June 1987)

STREGASCHLOSS, ARGYLL AND BUTE

This property, three miles from the little Highland town of Auchenlochtermuchty (pop. 786) commands one of the finest views of the Kyles of Mhoire Ochone. Set in 500 acres of ancient forest and flanked by the wild beauty of the Bengormless mountain range, the house itself is an architectural gem.

Built c. 1400 on the Austrian model, it boasts several turrets, a moat (the drawbridge was used as firewood during the oil crisis of 1732) and a particularly fine example of a dungeon, seldom seen in properties of this kind.

It has been owned by the clan Strega-Borgia since 1645, when it was acquired in lieu of rent by Malvolio di S'Enchantedino-Borgia from Campbell Caravanserus of Lochnagargoyle. Its charming and unusual name refers to the family's Italian heritage and the house's Germanic style of architecture.

(Rumour has it that the ghost of Malvolio's grandmother can still be seen in the wine cellar.)

The Ideal Candidate

From an upstairs window peered three pairs of eyes. The six eyes watched as a plump woman negotiated the moat, apparently unaware of the murderous Tock who dozed in its depths.

'That's the third one this week,' observed a voice.

'Fourth, if you count the one that Tock ate for breakfast,' said a second voice.

The third pair of eyes blinked. Too young to speak, their owner wondered if *this* one could change nappies and sing the right kind of lullaby to hush a witch baby to sleep.

Having spotted the sleeping crocodile as she crossed the moat, Mrs McLachlan climbed the steps, sat heavily on a stone gryphon guarding the front door and gazed around. She rooted in a battered handbag and produced a crumpled news-paper advert and a pair of reading glasses. Wedging the glasses on the end of her nose, she re-read:

> Energetic nanny/mother's help urgently required for Titus (12), Pandora (10) and Damp (14 months). The ideal applicant will enjoy a spot of light housework, be well versed in plumbing and veterinary science, have some understanding of cryogenics and know instinctively how to make chips that are crunchy on the outside and soft in the middle. Hours and salary negotiable.

'Take deep breaths, Flora,' Mrs McLachlan commanded herself. 'Relax. This is a perfectly ordinary job requiring no magical skills whatsoever. Think nanny. Think nappies. Think nursery teas, fluffy bunnies and lullabies . . .' She refolded the advert and tucked it back into her bag. 'You want to forget the past?' she continued. 'Here is your chance to put it behind you. From the moment you step through this door, you will forget that you were ever a witch.'

Above her head, the lintel was decorated with several cherubs peering through an infestation of stone bats. The ugliest of these cherubs had one eye that was not carved in stone, but rendered in black plastic, and this slid open, rotated slowly and finally fixed its lens on the woman below.

Upstairs in the observatory, Titus and Pandora

examined the new nanny on the CCTV screen. Damp crawled across the dusty floor, occasionally finding dead daddy-long-legs and popping them into her mouth.

'Let me see,' said Titus.

'I'm looking in her handbag just now, hang on, I'll move the field a bit.'

'Let me *see*,' said Titus.

'You're supposed to be watching Damp. I did for ages in the attic, it's your turn . . . oh gross!'

'What?'

'She's got hairy legs . . .'

'Could you stop giving me the picture in snack-sized bites? LET ME SEE.'

'She's nervous, Titus, see for yourself. Well, that's understandable.'

Pandora stood up and surrendered her seat to her brother. Titus pressed keys and rolled the mouse with the ease of an expert. The screen in front of him filled with a close-up of the wannabe-nanny's face.

'She's so *old*,' he moaned.

'Not as old as that wrinkly on Monday. Remember? The one that called me Pannetone and left lipstick kisses all over Damp?'

'Well, she was better than that scary one who went on about the importance of diet for raising children and said that if *she* got the job she'd make sure we ate Brussels sprouts and cabbage every other day.'

'Nightmare Nanny from Hell,' said Pandora.

'What does that make old furry-legs downstairs?' said Titus, allowing the screensaver to appear. A lurid pattern of purple bats flittering across a computer-generated landscape replaced the view of the ideal candidate downstairs.

'Come on, stinkpod,' he said, picking up his baby sister and opening the door for Pandora.

'She *hasn't*, has she?' Pandora glared at Damp.

'Oh yes, you have, haven't you, horrible? Phwoarrr . . .' Titus held Damp at arm's length. 'Let's go and meet Nanny, shall we?'

'Shall we dress up?' said Pandora. 'Flour in the hair? Lipstick blood? Fangs?'

'I suppose so,' said Titus, with little enthusiasm. 'Rats too?'

'Perfect,' Pandora called over her shoulder, as she ran downstairs holding her nose. 'Although Damp's *derrière* ought to be quite enough to put any nanny off.'

Titus followed downstairs, breathing through his mouth. He opened the kitchen door and sighed. Interviewing prospective nannies had been fun at first – introducing them to the pregnant rat, Multitudina, meeting Strega-Nonna in her deep-freeze, Tock the croc and all the other scream-inducing creatures that were part of life at StregaSchloss, but after one had watched the nannies turn pale and begin to twitch twenty times or more, the novelty and the glee began to pall.

Frankly, it was boring. Nannies were boring. Frightening them was boring, and listening to them try to ingratiate themselves with the family was mega-boring.

Titus watched as Pandora sprinkled flour in her hair in preparation for greeting the new nanny.

'Do we *have* to meet her?' Titus said, opening the fridge and gazing at the woeful lack of contents within.

'If we don't,' Pandora said in the voice used for explaining large ideas to small people with even smaller IQs, 'Mum might go ahead and hire her, and then we'd end up with someone as horrible as that one who said, "Much as it pains me to admit, children occasionally need to be spanked soundly for their own good."'

Titus slammed the fridge shut, and kicked it. Hard. 'I wonder if she tasted as bad as she sounded?' he said.

Pandora hauled Damp out of the compost bucket, scattered a handful of flour over the baby's head and smiled at her brother. 'Only Tock could answer that,' she said.

Upstairs the doorbell rang.

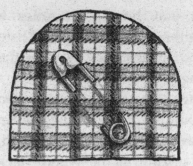

Latch Undone

With a sound that set his teeth on edge, Latch undid bolts, opened padlocks and turned a vast key in a rusty lock. 'You rang?' he said, stating the obvious.

Latch believed in wearing the classic butler's costume of white shirt, black tie and black jacket. Admiring his reflection in the hall mirror for the seventeenth time that morning, he thought how the overall effect was ruined by the sight of his own hairy knees peeking shyly from beneath a kilt of uncertain provenance.

He scratched furiously, for his butler's kilt had been pressed into service as a dog blanket before it became the uniform of a servant. In all other respects his job as Schloss-butler was perfect, for it gave him a large salary, use of a small Japanese car, three rooms in the Schloss attic and all in return for a pleasant manner with a door, being able to iron newspapers and balance the morning post on a silver tray – and wearing this unspeakable woolly skirt.

Scowling horribly, Latch opened the door. On the doorstep stood a woman. She was middle-aged, plump, carried a large handbag of battered plastic and smelled of lavender.

'Good morning,' she said, dragging her gaze upwards from Latch's knees to meet his eyes. 'I have an appointment with Mrs Borgia.'

Latch stared with a momentary lapse of manners. The woman's rolling 'R's sounded like the deep purr of a fireside cat and the lilt in her voice spoke of midges, peat bogs, sheep's wool ensnared in barbed wire and the underfoot resilience of heather. Latch was briefly transported back in time to his youth and then instantly hurled back into the present.

'Are you going to keep gawking at me like a scrapie sheep or are you going to let me in? Laddie?'

Latch cleared his throat, shuddered slightly and said, 'If Modom would be good enough to furnish me with her name?'

'Heavens, laddie, what a pompous little person you are. My name's Flora Morag Fionn Mhairi ben McLachlan-Morangie-Fiddach. Mrs McLachlan to youse. Now will you let me in?' And pushing past Latch, Mrs McLachlan strode into the great hall of StregaSchloss.

The morning sun highlighted the fact that the house had been sadly neglected. Cobwebs drooped across the ceiling, the crystal chandelier didn't twinkle and crumpled envelopes filled the empty marble fireplace. Breathing in the combined perfumes of beeswax and old dog with an undertone of log fire and full nappy, Mrs McLachlan came to a halt at a large hall table which was strewn with bills, letters, glossy catalogues, an assortment of leashes, ropes and chains and some exceedingly large dog collars.

Latch closed the front door, marched past Mrs McLachlan and threw open a door onto the darkest and most depressing room in StregaSchloss. 'The discouraging room, Modom. If you'll just take a seat, I'll inform Signora Strega-Borgia of your arrival.'

Latch bowed Mrs McLachlan into the cramped waiting room and closed the door on her. 'A McLachlan-Morangie-Fiddach!' he muttered. She'd probably brought her own kilt.

As the butler's footsteps receded down the corridor, Mrs McLachlan peered at the only seat in the discouraging room. This was a sofa which looked about as unwelcoming as it was possible to be without barbed wire, large signs saying KEEP OFF, and packs of patrolling Dobermans. Mrs McLachlan waited. A clock somewhere distant chimed the hour. Far away, a phone rang several times and stopped.

Mrs McLachlan prodded a sofa cushion and sighed. Despite her recent promise to herself, this was one of those times where just one little magical tweak would make life so much easier. With a furtive glance around herself to make absolutely sure that no-one could see what she was about to do, she opened her handbag. From deep inside it she removed a small perspex box. She undid a hidden clip and a tiny screen popped up, revealing a keyboard underneath. Hastily looking over her shoulder, she pinned her tongue between her teeth to aid concentration and typed in S.P.R.I.N.G.S., pressed a key named TRASH, re-typed G.O.O.S.E.-F.E.A.T.H.E.R. then pressed a key named REPLACE. She pointed the whole at the sofa and undid her tongue from her teeth.

There was a noise like that of someone being punched in the stomach with a vast marshmallow. A sort of *whufffff*. The sofa instantly looked like it had only just limped through three rounds with a heavyweight boxing champion. The sofa slumped, it bulged, it oozed saggily. Had it not been a sofa, it might have coughed and spat out a few broken teeth. Now it looked as if you could sit on it, without it putting up a fight.

Mrs McLachlan smiled. She replaced her perspex box in her handbag and sat heavily on the sofa. The sofa surrendered. A clock somewhere chimed quarter past the hour.

Hiring Flora

'**H**old *still*,' commanded Titus.

'I'm trying to,' said Pandora, 'but Damp wants to hold the lipstick ... No! *Damp!* Spit it *out*! Look at her, Titus, she looks like she fell from a great height and used her lips as a brake. Oh, Damp, don't dribble ...'

'What a disgusting baby,' said Titus lovingly. 'I think she's perfect for a bit of nanny-baiting, aren't you, Damp?' He stood back to admire the effect.

Damp's bottom lip quivered ominously.

'And now she's crying ... told you she'd be perfect,' Titus said, turning to grin at his mirrored reflection.

Pandora shifted Damp onto her other hip and gave the baby a half-eaten biscuit. Stopped in mid-wail by the appearance of food, Damp gazed up at her big sister then risked a look at Titus.

'You look *hideous*,' Pandora said approvingly.

Titus smirked, then hastily re-adjusted a set of glow-in-the-dark fangs, patted his slicked-down hair and pulled the collar of his cloak tight around his throat. 'This ought to do the trick,' he said.

'Exit one nanny,' Pandora agreed. 'Hold Small-and-Smelly till I sort out my veil.' She passed the baby over and began to drape her head and shoulders in tattered muslin. Damp made a grab for Titus's fangs.

'Move over, would you?' Pandora nudged her brother. 'Stop hogging the mirror.'

The three children gazed at their joint reflections. From the mirror, three small vampires gazed back.

'Ready?' Titus wrapped Damp securely in his cloak and opened the kitchen door.

'*Got* you.' Pandora plucked something off the kitchen table and instantly stuffed it down the front of her dress.

'Is that what I think it is?' groaned Titus. 'Oh, Pandora, you're so *gross*.'

'Yup,' said Pandora, gliding out of the kitchen in a swirl of muslin. 'Let's hope the new nanny thinks so too.'

Latch stood statue-still inside the door of the dis-couraging room, watching in disgust as his employer, Signora Strega-Borgia, fell under the spell of Mrs McLachlan ('*Call me Flora, dear*').

Signora Strega-Borgia was enchanted. At long last, here was a *normal* person. A person whose day would be full of nursery teas, changing nappies, singing lullabies and reading stories about happy families of fluffy bunnies. Stories in which Mother Rabbit wasn't a struggling student witch, and Father Rabbit hadn't hopped out of the burrow vowing never to return . . .

Three weeks ago, her husband, Signor Strega-Borgia, had stormed out of their family home in a temper and since then StregaSchloss had been shrouded in a veil of gloom. Despite the fact that their school was shut for the summer, the children rapidly turned mutinous, the staff grew surly and everyone spoke only in monosyllabic grunts. Dust and cobwebs began to accumulate, giving the whole Schloss an air of neglect. It was as if a fog had descended on the house – everything was coloured in shades of grey, and every day was a Monday.

Signora Strega-Borgia choked back a sob and peered hopefully at the woman in front of her. And there, now, in tweeds and sensible shoes sat an unlikely saviour. Here was Nanny McLachlan, who brought with her a blast of bracing Highland air, a gale that might sweep away dust and cobwebs, put a gleam back in the children's eyes and paint the colour back into all their lives. Or at the very least she would be able to rustle up a pan of chips that didn't cause the children to make gagging noises . . .

The sound of laboured breathing through the keyhole interrupted Signora Strega-Borgia's reverie. 'Latch, could you let the children in? I think it's time they met their new nanny.'

Latch opened the door with a tug, and Titus, Pandora and Damp fell into the discouraging room, thwarted in their attempts to eavesdrop.

'Get *off* me,' roared Pandora, 'you're tearing my veil!'

'My fangs are *caught* in your stupid veil, let go of my cloak!'

Squashed under her warring siblings, Damp began to wail.

'Poor wee mite,' said a voice, 'will she come to me? There, pet, what's this all over your face, och what a mess you're in.' Mrs McLachlan scooped Damp onto her lap, cradled her gently against her pillowy chests and stroked her baby-fluffed head. Damp felt warm and safe. She plugged her lipstick-smeared mouth with a well-sucked thumb, burrowed deeper into those chests, and fell fast asleep.

Hell's teeth, thought Latch, she's got the job.

'I've never seen Damp ever do that before,' said Signora Strega-Borgia in a reverential voice. 'Thank you, Mrs McLachlan. Now, Titus, Pandora, disentangle yourselves and meet your new nanny. This, my darlings, is Mrs McLachlan.'

'Hi,' said Pandora in a tone of colossal uninterest.

'Bride of Dracula?' said Mrs McLachlan. 'It's a bonny costume, dear, but did you know you've got a baby rat dangling from your bodice?'

'For heaven's sake, Pan!' roared Signora Strega-Borgia, losing her cool. 'Did you let Multitudina out with her brood again? How many times do I have to tell you that I take a very dim view of free-range rodents . . .'

'Mum! Don't start,' moaned Pandora.

'Count Dracula,' interrupted Mrs McLachlan, 'you have retrieved your teeth, I trust? Your fangs are back in the fold? Will we see you for a bite to eat later on?'

'Very funny,' muttered Titus, glaring at his shoes and avoiding eye-contact with this intruder.

'Titus . . .' warned his mother.

Slowly, as if he was wading through treacle wearing tennis rackets on his feet, Titus dragged himself across the carpet and extended a nail-bitten hand to shake. Mrs McLachlan's hand felt warm and soft. A definite improvement on the clammy-fish, nervous-nanny handshakes that Titus had been forced to endure of late. He risked a quick look. Mrs McLachlan's eyes met his and immediately crinkled up in a many-wrinkled smile. Titus shut his eyes like a clam and inwardly vowed never to grow old. He retrieved his hand and used it to re-adjust his slipping fangs.

'When could you start, Mrs McLachlan?' asked Signora Strega-Borgia.

'I already have, dear,' said Mrs McLachlan, patting the slumbering Damp.

'But your clothes? Personal effects?'

'Och, don't you worry about me, dear. I have everything I need in my bag.'

Something smells decidedly fishy, thought Latch, nobody travels *that* light.

'That's it, is it?' demanded Pandora. 'You're not even going to pretend to ask us if *we* like her?'

'You might have asked, you know,' added Titus reproachfully. 'I mean I know we don't pay her or anything, but we do count, don't we?'

'*We're* the ones that'll have to spend all our time with her while *you* vanish off to broomstick craft at the Institute of Advanced Spelling or whatever,' spat Pandora, fixing her mother with a look that could burn toast.

Signora Strega-Borgia groaned. Titus and Pandora had become decidedly prickly since their father had left and though Signora Strega-Borgia was becoming accustomed to their verbal spats, she found it deeply embarrassing to engage in all-out warfare in front of strangers, even if the strangers did invite one to call them Flora. 'Latch, would you show Nanny to the nursery while I have a word with the children? Do excuse us for a moment, Mrs McLachlan.'

'Call me Flora, dear.'

Trailing in their mother's wake, Titus and Pandora followed her along the corridor and out into the light of the kitchen garden. Birds sang, bees droned and a distant lawnmower stuttered, coughed and stalled. The brightness of the sunlight made Titus screw up his eyes and scowl fiercely. *She's going to tell us that Times Are Hard,* thought Titus. *Again. And how we all Have to Make Allowances. Again.*

Pandora glared at the bald baby rat she'd unpicked from her dress. *Bet your mother doesn't drag* you *out into the garden for A Word With The Children,* thought Pandora, *bet she just bites your ear and tells you to get on with chewing electrical cables.*

'Do you have to be quite so obnoxious?' hissed Signora Strega-Borgia. When no answer came, she dug deep in her pockets and produced a pair of secateurs. Picking on an innocent bay tree, she continued, 'Every single nanny.' *SNIP!* 'Not a smile, not even an attempt to be civil.' *SNIP!* 'You've made it perfectly plain . . .' *SNIP!* '. . . that you'd rather they all just dropped dead.' *SNIP!* 'What's so awful about this one?' *SNIP!*

'She's . . . old?' said Titus.

'So's Strega-Nonna,' said Signora Strega-Borgia, attacking the bay with renewed venom.

'But she's in the freezer and she's part of the family,' said Titus, desperately trying to think of more reasons not to hire Mrs McLachlan, 'and besides, Mrs McLachlan's *boring*. She won't know anything about computers, and she'll think Magic is some kind of oven cleaner.'

'Precisely,' snapped Signora Strega-Borgia, waving her secateurs for emphasis. 'The *last* thing this family needs is Nanny Magic or Nanny Modem. What we need is an ordinary, straight-forward, bedtime-at-nine and brush-your-teeth-a-hundred-times kind of nanny. And *that* is what we're about to get.'

'I don't want a nanny,' said Pandora, in a very small voice. The baby rat squeaked. Large salty wet things were dripping on its bald head. 'I don't want you to have to go out to work. I don't want you and Dad to get divorced. I want everything to be like it was before . . .'

Titus stared fixedly into the middle distance. Pandora had given voice to his deepest fear – she'd even *said* the D-word. His nose prickled and his vision blurred. No-one had mentioned divorce before . . . He silently willed his sister to stop. Whatever she was saying, he didn't want to hear it.

'Oh my poor Pan,' said Signora Strega-Borgia drawing her daughter close and reaching for Titus's hand. 'I know this is a horrible time for you both – you're missing your father dreadfully . . .'

Pandora looked up into her mother's face. In a voice devoid of any hope whatsoever she said, 'But do *you* miss Dad?'

Titus froze. Pandora had done it again. Somehow she'd reached into his head and plucked out the very question he didn't dare look at, far less *say*. His breath turned to ice in his lungs.

Signora Strega-Borgia's face crumpled, her eyes spilling tears and her mouth turning into a downward curve of anguish. 'Yes,' she whispered, 'every moment of every day. Every breath I take . . .' Her self-control dissolved in a flood of tears.

Titus exhaled in relief. Pandora's eyes shone. Signora Strega-Borgia hugged her children tight and in return four arms held her close and four hands patted her shoulders, stroked her face and wiped away her tears. Unnoticed, the baby rat made a bolt for freedom, loudly squeaking its disapproval of bipeds that leak.

A Little Bit of Damp

D amp was impressed. This new nanny could change a mean nappy, sing a tuneful (if wobbly) lullaby and didn't slobber at all when dishing out kisses. She'd watched Mrs McLachlan folding nappies and vests and had noted with approval the new nanny's command of nursery etiquette. Teddies were stacked neatly on shelves, books were arranged in diminishing order of height, and all broken toys were placed in a basket for future repair. Damp's tummy was full, her nappy dry and her head happily full of recently read stories. Now Mrs McLachlan sat in a sunlit corner of the nursery and mended socks.

Unobserved, Damp crawled purposefully towards Mrs McLachlan's handbag. She pulled at a corner of the bag and it slowly toppled over, spilling some of its contents on the nursery floor. The baby sat back on her bottom and began to explore.

There was a book of the kind that Bigs read, no pictures, lots of pages; no, don't want that, TOSS. There was a lipstick in a cracked plastic tube; no, did lipstick earlier, don't want that, FLING. There was a box that hummed quietly to itself. Intrigued, Damp reached out to pick it up. It felt warm as it vibrated gently in her hands. Turning it over, all the better to investigate, Damp unwittingly undid the latch. The box opened, exposing the keyboard within. Ahhhh. A piano-thing, thought Damp, prodding the keys.

QWERTYUIOP appeared on the screen, followed by a prompt, EXCUSE ME?

Damp pressed on, and produced !@£$%^&&& and unknown to her, the box responded, I DON'T THINK SO.

To Damp's astonishment, the background hum turned into a loud shriek. Damp dropped the box and did what any sensible baby would do in the circumstances. She threw back her head, opened her mouth and howled.

It worked. Mrs McLachlan responded instantly. 'You poor wee thing. What's the matter, pet? Did something in Nanny's bag bite you?'

Damp flapped at the piano-thing, now appearing to be having a temper-tantrum on the shiny floorboards.

'Ah.' Mrs McLachlan paled. 'You've met Nanny's make-up box. And my heavens, it's having hysterics . . .' She picked up the box and pressed a key. Instantly the shrieks stopped, the lid snapped shut, and the faint humming sound resumed. 'It won't harm you. Really. Let's put it away, out of sight, out of mind, shall we, and Nanny's book and her lipstick, then you can show me round your house? You lead with the crawl and I'll follow doing the breast-stroke.'

Damp set off, followed by Mrs McLachlan.

Night drew in at StregaSchloss. The wood pigeons fell silent, the air grew cool, and in the kitchen garden, the snipped bay tree wept tears of sap. A trickle of woodsmoke from the Schloss chimneys slowly dwindled to a thin line, etching a message of embers and ash across the night sky. Bats flittered out from their attic roost, their wings beating a leathery tattoo through the mist rolling in from the sea loch.

In the stillness of the moat, Tock ate an ornamental goldfish by way of a nightcap, belched a series of underwater bubbles, and dozed, dreaming of nannies and one-armed pirate snacks.

In the Schloss kitchen, Marie Bain, the French cook, blew her nose, examined the result in her handkerchief and sneezed wetly into tomorrow's soup. She turned out the lights, hunched her shoulders closer to her scrawny neck and sneaked along the passage and upstairs to her meagre attic bedroom. In her stained apron she carried three cheese-and-pickle sandwiches and two cookery books, in case sleep was slow in arriving and famine struck in the hours before dawn.

In the dungeons below the moat, lumbering shapes wheezed and scratched. Chains rattled, clanked and were still. In the background a steady drip of water on stone tapped out the night-time like a subterranean clock.

In the wine cellar, a large freezer ticked and hummed. Deep within, in her bed of permafrost, Strega-Nonna dreamt of polar bears, creaking icebergs and of the luminous shifting curtain of the Aurora Borealis.

Upstairs, propped up on pillows, soundly asleep in a full-length white nightgown, Mrs McLachlan snored. She slept too deeply to hear the traffic of fat little knees and hands, padding across the nursery floor in search of comfort.

Damp had awoken with silent fingers of mist pressed against the windows of the nursery. It was as if the sea loch had risen out of its bed and come to visit the Schloss, to peer in the windows and gaze damply at the sleepers within. Damp felt cold. She poked teddy after teddy through the bars of her cot, and, using her activity centre as a step, vaulted over the top rail and crash-landed onto the teddy mat below.

The corridor between the nursery and Signora

Strega-Borgia's bedchamber was long and dark. Damp crawled by Braille, feeling her way along the carpet till she reached her destination. She paused in the doorway and removed several dustballs from her pyjamas then crawled at speed into the bedroom. With an effort Damp hoisted herself onto her mother's bed and tunnelled under the sheets to reach the sleeping Mummy-hummock.

'Bog off, Damp,' groaned Pandora. 'Take your foot *out* of my nose.'

Damp climbed over Pandora and poked the next sleeping body hopefully.

'Horrible baby,' said Titus. 'Take your nappy *off* my face.'

Ignoring her siblings, Damp prised her mother's eyelids apart to check if she really was asleep. Two bloodshot eyes glared at her.

'You're hogging the quilt,' complained Titus.

'I'm about to fall off the edge of the bed,' whined Pandora.

'For heaven's sake!' exploded Signora Strega-Borgia. 'Whose bed is this, anyway?'

Damp smiled into her mother's face and settled happily in the middle of the bed. Her mother sighed. It was obvious that the baby thought that the bed belonged to her. Signora Strega-Borgia smoothed the quilt over Pandora's shoulder, tucked a wayward strand of hair behind Titus's ear and curled herself around Damp's small body. Around her, the children slept, safe in her bed, just as they had done since their father had disappeared. And just as she had done for the previous twenty-one nights, Signora Strega-Borgia lay awake staring at the ceiling, tears tracking silently down her face as she wondered for the millionth time where her husband had gone.

Where on Earth?

In a grey prison cell, a long way from home, Signor Luciano Strega-Borgia, father to Pandora, Titus and Damp, temporarily estranged husband of Signora Baci Strega-Borgia, woke up with a shriek. 'AAAAAAARGH!' And then, for he had a headache of monumental nastiness, 'Aaaa . . . oww . . . shhhhhhhh.'

His eyes roamed around his cell, taking in his floor-level view of four stone walls, one slatted bench, one solid door with peephole and lock, rather too many ceiling-mounted lightbulbs searing his eyes and what looked ominously like a potty within olfactory range of where he lay.

Things were not looking good, he decided, slowly getting onto all fours and then gently easing his stiff limbs onto the slatted bench. It *was* a potty.

This is a prison cell. This thing throbbing and pounding on the end of your neck is a head. Use it, Luciano. Think back, he commanded himself, what was the last thing you remember?

He'd been in a huff for some reason, stomping along the little lane that connected StregaSchloss with the main road to Auchenlochtermuchty. It was raining, he recalled, which was why . . .

He was momentarily distracted by the sight of a cockroach climbing out of the potty and pausing on the rim for a spot of grooming. To his disgust it appeared to be smacking its tiny lips.

. . . which was why he'd been only too glad to accept a lift from the driver of the black Mercedes who'd stopped to ask for directions. The car's windows were made out of dark-tinted glass, so he'd been unaware . . .

The cockroach keeled over and, with an almost inaudible splash, fell backwards into the potty.

. . . that sitting in the back of the car was a man dressed in black, gun lying casually in his lap, beckoning him inwards with a full hypodermic syringe which was promptly emptied into his arm . . .

. . . which would explain the pounding headache and brain-fuzz that made his recall of events so much more difficult. So, that was how, but where was he now? And why? And who? *Who* had kidnapped him? He had the sneaking suspicion that whoever it was did not have his best interests at heart.

This opinion was further reinforced by a ghastly

scream from somewhere outside Signor Strega-Borgia's cell door. 'NO NO NO, scusi Don Borgia, I so sorry I overcook da pasta, I never never do eet again. On my mama's grave I swear I never turn eet into stewed knitting ever again, NOOOOOOOO. AAAARGHHHHHH. Not the sharks! NOOOO!'

And, disturbingly, another voice, a vaguely familiar voice, 'Act like a man, Ragu. Pull yourself together, it's not the sharks, stupido, it's the piranhas, haa haa haaa.'

Signor Strega-Borgia turned pale and began to shake. *Don Borgia? Don Lucifer di S'Embowelli Borgia?* The most evil, heartless, amoral being ever to walk the earth? The man whose idea of a noble deed was to help little old ladies cross motorways into the path of oncoming traffic? Whose idea of entertainment was rounding up stray cats and cooking them in a microwave? Whose childhood had been spent in torturing his half-brother – his half-brother Luciano Strega-Borgia – who was currently sobbing his eyes out on a grey prison-cell floor and begging a drowned cockroach to exchange lives with him?

Yes. That Don Lucifer di S'Embowelli Borgia, and none other.

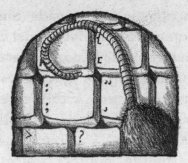

E-rats

L ife goes on, as it always has. Worlds collapse, people go to war, divorce and cause each other immense amounts of grief, but nappies still have to be changed, food cooked and parents, no matter how unhappy, still have to go to work.

Thus it was at Strega-Schloss. Mrs McLachlan settled in, Damp fell in love with her and Titus and Pandora had to admit grudgingly that her chips were indeed crunchy on the outside and soft in the middle.

Signora Strega-Borgia bid the children a tearful farewell and set off to complete her degree in advanced witchcraft, returning to StregaSchloss at weekends.

In the absence of her mother, Pandora opened

Multitudina's cage door and allowed her pet rat the freedom of StregaSchloss. By default, this freedom was also granted to Multitudina's thirteen off-spring.

Seizing the opportunity to unlock the secrets of his absent father's vast computer, Titus moved the entire system out of Signor Strega-Borgia's study and into his own bedroom.

With these two seemingly unconnected actions, Titus and Pandora unwittingly set off a chain reaction of events that would prove to be cata-strophic. This is how it began.

Damp had done A Bad Thing. Damp knew it was A Bad Thing because Mrs McLachlan's mouth had shrunk to a flat tight line, and her eyes had grown cold and wee.

Minutes before, Damp had been gazing in adora-tion at the open disk drawer on Titus's CD-ROM. Above the disk drawer sat Titus's modem with its two buttons decorated with stick-on eyeballs. Titus had applied these from a sheet of cut-out face parts, and thus it was hardly surprising that Damp put two and two together and arrived at pi r squared.

It's a *face*, thought Damp delightedly, what a *big* mouth, all the better to eat breakfast with. She crawled closer to the CD-ROM.

Hello face, she thought, waving some bacon rinds that she'd found on the floor. Want some breakfast? She clambered onto Titus's desk, using its open drawers as steps, waving the bacon rinds like a flag. The open CD drawer gaped hungrily. Nice face, decided Damp, have some breakfast. With small baby fingers, Damp stuffed her bacon rinds, one by one, into Titus's CD-ROM.

It was thus that Mrs McLachlan found her. 'Damp! NO! Stop right NOW!' she commanded.

Uh oh, thought Damp. She paused in her bacon-stuffing efforts and, at a loss for what to do next, popped her thumb into her mouth and simultaneously risked a quick glance at her beloved nanny. What she saw was not cheering. Instead of radiating Highland warmth and pillowy comfort, Mrs McLachlan's whole being smacked of cold rain showers and grim mountain peaks.

Mrs McLachlan bristled, pursed and tsked. 'Right, girlie,' she said, plucking Damp off Titus's desk, 'you're coming where I can keep an eye on you, but first, a nappy change.'

Sorry, face, thought Damp, as she was hauled inelegantly bathroomwards. Bye bye, face.

The enticing reek of bacon rinds slowly congealing inside the CD-ROM turned it into an olfactory beacon, sending out a clear signal to those creatures that relied on their noses for survival. Several such creatures, thirteen to be exact, were idly chewing paper under Titus's bed when the first finger-like waft of bacon arrived. Thirteen noses twitched. The fourteenth nose snored, attached to Multitudina, rat-mother to multitudes, who was catching up on some well-earned sleep while her brood amused themselves with an irreplaceable stack of pre-war *National Geographic* magazines. Thirteen noses found bacon to be a far more exciting prospect, foodwise, than paper and ink. Fifty-two pink paws stampeded for the enticements of the CD-ROM, squeaking and snapping at each other in their haste to be first at the feast.

Multitudina awoke to see the last of her children's bald tails snaking to and fro, dangling twitchily from the open drawer of the CD-ROM.

'Hell's teeth!' she squeaked, lunging after her offspring and gaining the desktop as the last millimetre of tail vanished into the grey gape of the drawer. Despite a rigorous post-natal exercise programme, Multitudina had not managed to regain her skinny pre-pregnancy figure, and found herself unable to squeeze through the gap and rescue her children. Wild squeakings from within informed her that her children were quite happy, thank you very much, and didn't intend ever coming back out to eat paper with Mum. Having scoured the CD-ROM of bacon rinds and congealed fat, they'd found a way into another grey slot and were checking it out for more of the same. The thirteen squeakings grew fainter as Multitudina's brood investigated Titus's adjoining modem.

Multitudina squatted on the keyboard to have a think about what to do next, depressing several keys under her bottom as she considered the problem. Behind her, the screen sprang to life. A dialogue box appeared, saying SEND? Multitudina scratched an itch on her hindquarters, and unknown to her, depressed several keys simultaneously. MESSAGE SENT flashed briefly.

Abruptly the squeaking stopped. Multitudina stopped scratching and sniffed the air. The babies were gone. Here one minute and gone the next. What was a mother to do? She heaved a sigh of relief. Peace at last, she thought, and plenty more where they came from. She leapt off the desk, scuttled under the bed and began chewing up the May 1935 edition in preparation for her next brood.

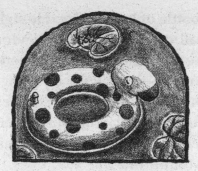

The Wager

'**T**itus, I'm in deep shtuch.' Pandora collapsed on her brother's bed with a small wail.

Titus didn't respond, unless a grunt counted as an expression of filial concern.

'Listen up, Titus, I need your help.'

'I'm busy,' came the reply.

Pandora unfolded herself from the bed and came to stand by her brother. Titus muttered and tapped on a keyboard, seemingly oblivious to the presence of his sister.

'I can't tell where that stupid computer ends and you begin. Titus, if you don't stop and listen to me, I'm going to see if *it* likes Coke as much as you do.'

Titus unglued his eyeballs from the screen and looked up. Pandora was unscrewing the cap from a vast bottle of brown fizz. He sighed.

'Ah! Eyeball contact,' gloated Pandora. 'Is there intelligent life on Planet Titus? Yes, there appears to be a large amoeba-thing with an open hole in the middle of its head, but we are experiencing some difficulty in establishing communication.'

Titus sighed again. 'What *is* it?' he said.

'I've lost Multitudina.'

'Big deal,' said Titus, 'plenty more rats where she came from.'

Pandora glared at her brother. 'And all her babies, Titus – all thirteen of them.'

'They'll turn up,' said Titus philosophically. 'Floating in the soup, down the toilet, hot-wired to the back of the fridge . . .'

'Titus. I shut them in *here*. Before breakfast. And when I came back upstairs with their bacon rinds, they were gone.'

'What did you do with the bacon rinds?' asked Titus irrelevantly.

'Damp probably ate them. But that's not the point, the point is . . .'

'The point *is*,' said Titus, 'that this is *my* bedroom, and *you* introduced fourteen free-range rats, several bits of dead pig and one incontinent baby into *my* space. Without *my* permission. *That's* the point.'

'Your Highness. Accept my humble apologies. Entering your Royal Bedchamber without permission is a crime punishable by death, but, sire, I can account for said bits of bacon and smelly baby – one is inside the other, and both are in the nursery – but where are Multitudina and her tribe?'

'You're toast, Pandora,' said Titus. 'Mum'll be back tonight and when she finds out . . .'

'Titus . . .' groaned Pandora. '*Please* . . .'

'I don't like rats, remember? Frankly, I'm delighted that your disgusting rodent's done a runner.'

'She's *not* disgusting.'

'She's a foul-mouthed, yellow-fanged smelly bit of vermin that's probably into cannibalism.'

'She did *not* eat her babies, Titus. You've got to help me find them.'

'If you're so brilliant, *you* find them.'

'Bet I can,' said Pandora.

'Bet you can't.'

'How much?'

'A game of Monopoly?' said Titus with faint hope.

'*NEVER*,' yelled Pandora. 'Frankly I'd rather swim a lap across the moat than play with *you*.'

'Big words, big deal, Pandora. You're all talk and no action. Inside you're just a fluff-brained *girl*. You'd never *dare*.'

Livid with rage, Pandora forgot to engage her brain before opening her mouth. 'I bet I CAN find her,' she shrieked. 'AND I WOULD TOO DARE! AND I'M NOT JUST *TALKING*!'

'No,' agreed Titus, 'you're shouting. And your eyes have gone all funny.'

'I'm not SHOUTING,' Pandora insisted. 'I'll find Multitudina or I'll swim the moat. *Done*. Satisfied?'

'You're kidding,' gasped Titus. 'You can hardly swim, let alone fight off crocodiles.'

'You're the one who needs armbands and a rubber ring, Titus,' her voice wobbled dangerously. 'And when I say done, I mean it.'

Despite her bluster, reality was dawning. What on earth was she doing, agreeing to swim across the moat? Tock was starving. Ravenous. Hadn't eaten a nanny for at least a fortnight. 'I mean it, Titus, but . . .'

'Ah! I knew there would be a but. No, you can't wear a suit of armour to swim in. Tock hates tinned food and, no, you may not feed Tock an elephant before you begin.'

'You seem awfully confident that I won't find Multitudina's ratettes.'

'You could say that,' Titus said smugly. 'But before you ask, I haven't touched them, harmed them or even seen the ghastly beasts since last night. Now . . . *but* what?'

'But . . . I need a week to find them.'

'Three days.'

'Five days, then. Come on, Titus, play fair.'

'In five days that disgusting rat-slob could produce another litter.'

46 ——

'Give me five days to find the missing babies, and if I don't I'll swim the moat,' said Pandora, crossing her fingers tightly.

'Deal,' said Titus.

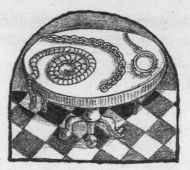

Beasts in the Basement

Damp sat tethered in her high chair, watching Mrs McLachlan prepare dinner. In a corner of the Schloss kitchen, Latch ironed the current edition of the *Financial Times* and Marie Bain stuck out her tongue at her reflection in the mirror.

'Ees no goot,' she decided, 'Meesuss McCacclong, I not feel well.'

'Never mind, dear,' said Mrs McLachlan vaguely. 'Just give me a hand with these chopped livers, and then you can have a wee lie down.'

Marie Bain reluctantly dragged herself away from the mirror and came over to the table where Mrs McLachlan stood stirring, wrist deep in gore, adding cubes of bloody jelly to a vast cauldron full of wriggling pinkness. Marie Bain's eyes widened as she beheld the contents of the cauldron.

Mrs McLachlan smiled kindly as she scooped out a heaving spoonful and offered it to the glassy-eyed cook.

'Now *you're* the expert, dear,' she said ingratiatingly. 'I don't know if I've put enough salt in. Have a wee taste and tell me what you think?'

Marie Bain turned an unbecoming shade of green, and with a gargle like a drain coming finally unblocked, leant over the cauldron and was copiously sick within.

Damp covered her eyes with her hands and gave a small moan. Latch rolled his eyes heavenwards and pressed on, thankful that someone had at last passed comment on the merit of Mrs McLachlan's current culinary offering. Nasty foreign muck, why didn't she stick to what she was good at, like chips? Still . . . at least *he* wouldn't have to eat it. Not now.

Mrs McLachlan tsked and stirred in Marie Bain's contribution. 'If you think so, dear,' she said, utterly unflappable. 'Still, myself, I would have added a teeny bit more salt. Let's see what the wee pets think, shall we?'

The nanny swept past Damp, kicked open the door to the dungeon and disappeared downstairs, calling, 'Wakey wakey. Dinnertime. Here's Nanny with some tasty numns for the wee pets.'

The dungeon was home to Knot, the yeti, Sab, the gryphon and Ffup, the dragon, none of whom qualified even remotely for the collective title of 'wee pets'. For a start, they were enormous.

Ffup, not fully grown, was the size of a stretch limousine and expected, in adulthood, to attain the dimensions of an average bungalow. Knot was eight feet of hulking matted hairiness and Sab resembled a leather lion with wings. For the previous six hundred years they had functioned admirably, if a tad erratically, as forms of guard-dog, patrolling the acres around StregaSchloss and devouring intruders. More recently, with the advent of the postal service and the consequent daily visits by postmen and other unplanned deliveries, the Strega-Borgias had decided that it might be safer to keep the beasts under some form of control. Hence the ropes, chains and leashes on the hall table, and the need for cages in the dungeon.

They gathered in the gloom, nostrils a-quiver, united in their disdain for Mrs McLachlan's offering.

'What d'you call this slop?' roared Ffup, snorting twin bursts of fire through the bars of his cage. Sab flapped leathery wings in a menacing fashion and spat onto the dungeon floor.

Undaunted, Mrs McLachlan unlocked the cage door and edged inside, dragging the brimming cauldron behind her. 'I'll have none of that adolescent nonsense, Ffup, and as for you, Sab, didn't your mother teach you never to spit?'

A stunned silence greeted her query. Didn't she

understand that she was supposed to run away screaming for help, not deliver a lecture on correct behaviour? Knot shuffled forwards, his matted hair clotted with the festering remains of many dribbled dinners. He dipped a paw into the cauldron and was just about to have an exploratory lick when Mrs McLachlan grabbed both his paws, turned them palm upwards and tsked mightily. 'I thought so . . .' she said grimly. 'Upstairs with you, and wash those paws properly before dinner. What d'you think you are, a wild animal?'

Knot burst into tears and shuffled blindly upstairs.

'Me too,' yelled Ffup. 'I haven't washed my claws for at least 600 years.' The dragon leapt after Knot, trailing little plosive puffs of smoke in his wake.

Sab folded his wings over his eyes, and turned to stone.

'Not hungry, pet?' enquired Mrs McLachlan solicitously, ladling her stew into three metal troughs. From upstairs, an earsplitting scream shattered the subterranean calm of the dungeon. Mrs McLachlan sighed. One of Marie Bain's many peccadilloes was her inability ever to come to terms with sharing a roof with the beasts. 'Pull yourself together, dear,' shouted Mrs McLachlan. 'They're more frightened of you, than you are of them . . .'

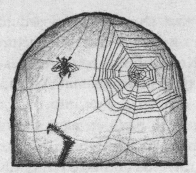

Arachnids in the Attic

Pandora lifted the lid of the chest freezer and bailed out several boxes of fish fingers, a tray of profiteroles and three half-eaten tubs of ice-cream.

Strega-Nonna lay at the bottom of the freezer, her small body wrapped in twelve layers of aluminium foil, her head framed in a ghostly halo of frosty white hair.

'Nonna,' whispered Pandora, 'you haven't seen Multitudina around, have you?'

'There's not much of a view inside here,' came the faint reply, and, 'Shut the lid, child, you're letting the heat in.'

Heck, thought Pandora, dropping the lid on her great-great-great-great-great-great-grandmother's tomb. What now? Four-and-a-half days left, and not a rat-dropping to be found. Sighing heavily, and abandoning the fish fingers, profiteroles and ice cream on the floor of the wine cellar, Pandora trekked up eight flights of stairs to the Schloss attic, a vast family museum of a loft space, full of dust and cobwebs, home to generations of spiders, woodworms and roosting bats. It was stuffed to the eaves with ancestral memories of Borgias long gone: several hundred oil paintings of family members, trunkloads of love letters, death threats and ancient shopping lists, a stableful of outgrown rocking horses, eight canary cages in varying stages of collapse, and, spanning the entire length of the attic, a teetering mountain range of magazines and books.

Pandora raised the heavy trap-door and climbed in. Light filtered through ropes of spiderweb, picking out what appeared to her to be an absolute rat-Mecca. A million places to hide, a million things to chew and a million ways to make sure your mistress has to do a synchronized swim with a ravening reptile.

'Come on, Multitudina,' she croaked, trying to sound enticing through a throatful of dust.

Nothing stirred.

'This is no place to raise a family,' she tried, hoping to appeal to the rodent's dismaying lack of maternal instincts. Several spiders paused in their spinning, debated whether to argue with this hairless biped, and decided against it. 'PLEASE COME

BACK,' Pandora yelled. 'MY LIFE DEPENDS ON IT!'

She slumped onto a nearby trunk, sending a cloud of dust motes spiralling upwards. From a window came the frantic buzz of a fly attempting to unglue itself from a web. Hypnotized, Pandora watched the fly grow more agitated, its wing-beat becoming an invisible blur, the pitch of its buzzing rising to the insect equivalent of a shriek. The web sagged under the weight of a monstrous spider whose abdomen was the size of a tennis ball, suspended on legs that cried out for shaving foam and a good razor. The spider wore bright pink lipstick, expertly applied round its mouthparts – a subtlety not lost on its intended victim, the pitch of whose buzzing reached an agonizing high C.

'Oh for heaven's sake, can't you die with dignity?' snapped the spider, impatiently tweaking the web tighter.

The fly fell silent, save for the odd whimper.

'Tarantella!' cried Pandora.

'The very same,' replied the spider.

'Pet lamb,' said Pandora, with total disregard for species, 'I haven't seen you for ages.'

Tarantella grinned widely and popped a fly wing into her mouth. She crunched, swallowed and extended a hairy leg to pat Pandora on the hand.

'So, what brings you up here?' she asked, licking her lips with a small black tongue. Pandora found herself mesmerized by Tarantella's tongue, as it sought out every tiny uneaten flake of wing, transferring each minute morsel into her maw and devouring them . . .

'I've lost Multitudina,' she said.

The spider shut her mouth with a snap. 'Good riddance to bad rattish,' she muttered. 'And before you even think it – NOT GUILTY.'

'Have you seen her, though?' persisted Pandora.

'Not up here. Not in my domain, thank you. I'd bite her if I caught sight of so much as a whisker.'

'I've made a bet with Titus that I'll find her,' said Pandora miserably.

'A wager?' squeaked the spider, rubbing all eight of her legs together with glee. 'What's the prize?'

'Nothing much, just fourteen rats and the privilege of staying alive . . .'

'And the forfeit?' the spider's mouth gathered into a fuschia-pink O of horror.

'Swimming the moat,' said Pandora.

'Auuuuk,' squawked Tarantella, remembering several highly unpleasant encounters with water, and ever mindful of the legendary Incy-Wincy's watery fate.

'. . . with Tock,' added Pandora.

'Oh, what a tangled web . . .' groaned Tarantella sympathetically.

'I'm in a real mess,' agreed Pandora. 'Any ideas where that elusive rodent could be?'

The spider fell silent, meditatively twirling a skein of silk around one leg. Her doomed dinner began to thrash from side to side in an attempt to break free, buzzing and wailing as it did so. 'How am I supposed to think with that racket going on?' snapped Tarantella, unwrapping the trapped fly and stinging it into silence. 'My guess would be anywhere near food. And being a disgusting rat, the older and mouldier the food, the better.' She paused to sip the liquid part of the fly from its carapace. 'So much more civilized, we spiders, fresh food is far healthier . . .'

Pandora watched in fascinated disgust as the spider sucked the fly dry.

'Now, where do we find rotten food?' continued Tarantella, warming to her theme between slurps. 'We find it overlooked under sinks, fridges, freezers and cookers. We find it in trash buckets, wheelie bins and waste baskets. However, these days we also find it in hospitals, schools and old people's homes . . .'

'Thanks,' interrupted Pandora, desperately trying to avoid a Tarantella-Tirade. 'Heavens, is that the time? Golly, must dash.'

She backed away, waving limply as the spider continued.

'Incidentally in aeroplanes, prisons and nasty foreign kitchens . . .' Tarantella ran out of locations as Pandora slid through the trapdoor. 'Don't you worry,' she called, waving goodbye with all eight legs. 'Between us we'll find her. I've friends in high places. I'll put out some feelers . . .'

At Home with the di S'Embowellis

Pronto, right-hand man to Don di S'Embowelli Borgia, knocked on the door of his master's study and entered, gliding inwards as if on oiled wheels. The Don was bellowing down the telephone, his back to the door, unaware of Pronto's silent arrival.

'You're telling me that the New York sector is down as well?'

A tiny voice on the other end squeaked and shrilled, bleating excuses and apologies.

'I don't care what time it is there, *nobody* sleeps unless I say so – unless they want to sleep with the fishes investigating their concrete overshoes. Do I make myself clear?'

The faraway voice chittered nervously.

Pronto risked a respectful cough. 'Maestro?'

The Don swung round to glare at him.

'Your half-brother, Maestro.'

The Don barked a hideous Latin threat into the receiver and slammed it back in its cradle. 'What about him?' he spat.

'It's time. We've had him locked up for a month. He's demanding better food and a telephone to call his lawyer. We've hosed him down, given him a shave and he's downstairs, waiting for you, Maestro.'

Shackled to a bronze throne in the middle of a vast chamber in his half-brother's Palazzo, Luciano Strega-Borgia gazed around himself in a state of total bewilderment.

Over the years, his contact with his half-brother had deteriorated: Lucifer hardly ever replied to Christmas cards or e-mails, his Omerta-like silence giving rise to much speculation on Signor Strega-Borgia's part as to the murderous nature of his half-brother's business dealings. Still . . . for a simple Italian killer, Lucifer had done well for himself. Signor Strega-Borgia's first glimpse of the Palazzo mirrored in a cypress-rimmed lake had filled him with amazement. A brief hobble in leg irons along marble corridors had brought him to this opulent room where he caught his reflection staring back at himself from hundreds of gilt-framed mirrors. Massive portraits of Borgias long-dead lined the walls. His eye fell on an oil painting of a spectacularly ugly man with a nose of Titanic girth, a nose that reminded Luciano of the nasal appendage of an elephant . . .

With an earsplitting crash, a far door flew open, and in strode Don Lucifer di S'Embowelli Borgia. As usual, his nostrils entered the room at least three seconds ahead of the rest of his body. Luciano stood up to greet his long-lost half-brother. His legs shook, his outstretched hand trembled, and his voice emerged as a squeak. 'Lucifer, how . . . how nose to see you.' He had the faintest suspicion that this was not the best thing to say.

Don Lucifer glared at Luciano. He had half a mind to feed the moron to the piranhas immediately and forget the rest of the plan. But no. There was work to be done. And done quickly. He needed to persuade this lily-livered goose of a man to sign a will favouring him, Don Lucifer, and then . . . well . . . the piranhas were a little peckish . . .

Fixing his half-brother with a smile devoid of any warmth whatsoever, Don Lucifer kissed him on both cheeks. 'Baby brother. Little Luciano,' he hissed, 'I'm ssso glad we could drag you over here.'

Signor Strega-Borgia began to protest.

'But,' interrupted Don Lucifer, holding up his hands as if to ward off his half-brother's words, 'but, why, you must be ravenous. Something to eat, yes? PRONTO! Get the shark steaks on the barbecue NOW.' He produced a key from his pocket and with a twist of his wrist, freed Signor Strega-Borgia from the bronze throne. 'And now,' he said, cosily wrapping his arm around his half-brother's trembling shoulders, 'we have so much catching up to do. Your boy. Titus. The little runt, excuse me, the fine young man, why he must be what ten? eleven? Almost of an age to inherit Poppa's money, the stupid old, I mean, may he rest in peace . . .'

'Twelve, actually,' muttered Signor Strega-Borgia, 'twelve years since . . .'

. . . Lucifer and Luciano last met on the night of their father's death, in the crowded bedroom where the old man lay, his heart running down like an overwound clock. Don Chimera had called his sons to his bedside where he was propped up on pillows, saying his farewells. Around him were the eleven Mafia Dons (who, together with Don Chimera, divided and ruled the underworld), three lawyers and an assortment of mayors, police chiefs and politicians who had come to bid their old friend goodbye.

In the background, a nurse fluffed pillows, smoothed sheets and made her patient as comfortable as possible. The crowded room was stifling, full of the smell of fear and imminent death. Lucifer, immune to the heat, sat by the fireside, roasting chestnuts in the embers and eagerly waiting for his father's death rattle. Then, at long last he would become the new Don, Don Lucifer di s'Embowelli Borgia, eldest son of the recently departed Don Chimera di Carne Borgia. Chestnuts had never tasted so sweet.

Lucifer happily planned his first day in power: item first, he thought, dispose of dumb half-brother.

Item second, buy that Porsche he'd dreamed of ever since the words brrm brrm *had crossed his lips.*

Item third, computerize the gambling, drug-running and extortion rackets that had made Don Chimera his millions.

Item fourth, bulldoze this old ruin and find a Palazzo.

Item fifth, find a good plastic surgeon for his nose.

Item sixth, ask that gorgeous nurse to marry him.

Item seventh . . .

The door to his father's bedchamber burst open, revealing his sobbing half-brother with a tiny baby in his arms.

'Poppa!' cried Luciano. 'I came as soon as I heard. Look, Poppa – I bring you your first grandchild!'

The sea of bodies parted to allow Luciano access to his father's bed. To a man, the assembled Dons, lawyers, mayors, police chiefs and politicians shuffled, coughed and examined their fingernails intently.

Holding out his bald infant to its grandfather, Signor Strega-Borgia said, 'Poppa, look the baby has your hair!'

The old man choked, spluttered and laughed like a blocked drain.

'Don't get him too excited, Signor,' cautioned the nurse. 'He's very frail.'

Don Chimera reached out, took his grandchild in his hands and tucked the baby safely in the crook of his arm.

'May I?' he wheezed.

'Please, Poppa – I'd be honoured.'

The old Don began to carefully unwrap his grandchild. The baby stopped crying and gazed solemnly at the old man.

'Look – I stop the crying. What have we here, little one? No clues here at all, only one white layer after another, no, the last one is not white, it is caca yellow, like your uncle Lucifer's eyes, no?'

By the fireside, Lucifer ground his teeth.

The baby's deep blue eyes never blinked as Don Chimera unwrapped the nappy and gazed within.

'A boy!' he crowed. 'My grandson . . . ?'

'Titus,' supplied the proud father.

The baby opened a mouth innocent of teeth, and bestowed upon his grandfather a smile of such infant perfection that the old Don seemed to rally a little. 'Signor Dombi, I have need of you.'

One of the lawyers detached himself from the crowd and came to the bedside. 'Maestro?'

'I wish to change my will in favour of my new grandson.'

'Poppa . . . there is no need,' interrupted Signor Strega-Borgia. 'Don't be so morbid, we'll have you better in a week or two.'

'Luciano, don't be ridiculous. In a week or two I'll be compost. Now, shut up and let me finish.'

The nurse drew Signor Strega-Borgia to one side and whispered in his ear.

'He's right, you know, Signor. Don't waste time arguing with him, just say goodbye properly, he won't see the night out.'

In the background they could hear the subdued murmur of the lawyer and the old Don, and the artificial silence caused by everyone in the room straining to overhear what it was they were discussing.

Lucifer sat stunned by the fireplace. This couldn't be happening to him.

That bald caca factory was going to inherit what was rightfully his? It was insufferable. Something had to be done. Don Chimera had to be stopped before the new will was written. He stood up, intending to call a halt to this nonsense.

It was at this point that two dozen forgotten roasting chestnuts exploded in a fusillade of what sounded remarkably like machine-gun fire. Instantly every man in the room dived for cover and simultaneously let rip with all the firepower at their disposal. All was chaos and screaming confusion. Windows shattered, wood splintered and feathers flew. For a minute nothing could be seen for plaster dust, gun smoke and duck down. As the air cleared, a figure appeared in the middle of the room, baby in arms, miraculously undamaged.

'Have you all taken leave of your senses?' it enquired in a voice hoarse with terror. 'Poppa needs peace and quiet . . .'

'He doesn't even need that, Signor,' muttered the nurse, emerging from behind a medicine cart. 'I'm afraid he's gone.'

With impeccable timing, the infant Titus began to cry.

*

Twelve long years had passed, then, mused Don Lucifer, propelling his half-brother towards the dining room. Twelve highly productive years of extortion, terror and many murders. Don Chimera's millions lay in a bank vault, entrusted to the care of the lily-livered Luciano, waiting for Titus to reach the age of thirteen. Don Chimera's will had specified that Titus would come into his inheritance as soon as he became a teenager, the dying grandparent believing that wealth was wasted on the old. Don Lucifer ground his teeth at the prospect of Titus inheriting anything. However, he thought, a smile playing round his mouth . . . if Luciano, in a fit of brotherly love, were to sign all the money over to Lucifer . . . and if Titus were to meet with some regrettable accident before his thirteenth birthday . . . well, that would be just . . .

'Excellent!' roared Don Lucifer, dropping Luciano into a chair in front of the laden dining table. 'What a feast for the prodigal brother, eh?'

Nil by Mouth

Mrs McLachlan was cold. The dungeons had that kind of effect on warm-blooded creatures, and trying to spoonfeed gryphons with dribbly ladlefuls of cold stew hadn't exactly helped.

She sat at the kitchen table trying to warm up over a cup of tea, watching Latch as he ironed the day's paper in readiness for Signora Strega-Borgia's return from the Advanced Witchcraft Institute.

'Anything of note in the news, dear?' she asked.

Latch looked up from the ironing board. 'I'm just doing the horoscope page if you're interested. When is your birthday, Mrs McLachlan?'

'Next week, Latch,' she answered sweetly, 'my thousandth actually. Do you think we'll have enough candles?'

'That makes you a Leo, doesn't it?' he said, un-deterred by her sarcasm. 'It says here, "Beware of unwelcome guests. Swift action is required to eliminate them."'

'The children must be going to catch head lice,' muttered Mrs McLachlan to herself.

Latch, oblivious, read on, '"A cool head will be required when all around are losing theirs" . . . how very mysterious, don't you think? Of course these horoscopes are all a load of codswallop, but some-times there's a grain of truth in what they say.'

'Will that be all, Latch?' said Mrs McLachlan, absentmindedly scratching her head.

'Take mine, for instance,' he continued, doggedly sticking to his theme. '"Immense courage will be required to achieve your goals, but a tendency to rush in where angels fear to tread could have amus-ing consequences." Well, I ask you, who wrote this garbage?' He threw down the paper, dumped the iron on the range next to a bubbling pan of sprouts, and folded the ironing board into a cupboard.

Marie Bain retrieved the paper and scanned the columns for her own horoscope. Against a backdrop of rising billows of sprout-scented steam, she re-sembled an apron-clad infernal ferret, her little eyes darting snakily along rows of type. Oblivious to the bubbling pans behind her, she read on.

Mrs McLachlan attempted to rescue the supper. 'Marie, dear, shall I drain the sprouts? They must surely be done by now.'

The cook's eyes barely rose above the newspaper. Turning slowly to the crossword page and producing a tiny pencil stub from the pocket of her apron, she replied. 'Another twenty-five meenots, Meesus McCacclong, then they be verr soft, chust how the Seenyora like them.'

Mrs McLachlan rolled her eyes heavenwards, and sat down heavily at the kitchen table. Latch bent over her shoulder and whispered, 'Eet ess writted in the stars, under the sign of Mush, the overcooked wegetable, that due to a planetary eclipse of the great star Sprout, and a hellish conjunction between the constellation Lumpy Spud and Leathery Haddock, that tonight might be a good time for a little clandestine chip-frying. What say you?'

'The stars never lie, Latch,' answered Mrs McLachlan. 'You peel and I'll sneak downstairs later and fry them.'

Up in the observatory, Titus was scanning the skies, looking for his mother. So far he'd spotted three passenger planes, their lofty vapour trails gradually dispersing in the lilac dusk. The crescent moon shone from the still waters of the moat, its reflection curled elegantly round a waterlily that was pulling its petals close against the night.

One by one, the stars became visible, linking dot by dot into recognizable constellations. Just as Titus had identified the Big Dipper, a wavering black dot appeared on the horizon.

Regular as clockwork, the waterlilies stirred as Tock's knobbly snout broke the surface of the moat, and with a series of rusty honks and creaks, the crocodile welcomed his mistress home. The black dot grew into a blot and then a shape, then a vaguely identifiable silhouette and ... 'Mum!' yelled Titus.

Signora Strega-Borgia was back.

By the time Titus had skidded down the nine flights of stairs that connected the observatory to the great hall downstairs, his mother was handing her broomstick keys over to Latch.

'Stick it in the workshop, would you, Latch?' she said, peeling off her leather flying helmet and tossing her gauntlets onto the hall table. 'I'll need you to have a look at it tomorrow. It's running very rough, and I nearly stalled over Edinburgh. Sticky moment there, damn thing started shedding twigs and coughing and spluttering over the Castle, *much* to the amusement of a crowd of American tourists, and I'm sure I've caught a cold from hanging around up there but we got here in the end ...'

Signora Strega-Borgia caught sight of her son, and ran forward to give him a huge hug. 'Dear Titus, how I've missed you,' she whispered into his hair. She smelled of engine oil and perfume, the fragrance of mothers returned from far away. Titus squeezed her tight, and then, after a moment, looked up at her beloved face. Two miniature reflections of himself stared back out of his mother's green eyes. 'Oh, Titus, I can't tell you – it's been *such* fun, but oh, how I've missed you all,' she said, wrapping one arm round his shoulders. 'Did you miss me?'

Latch coughed, and tactfully departed for broomstick parking duty.

'Every night,' said Titus truthfully. 'Your bed was empty, and Mrs McLachlan said we could come into hers, but she *snores.*'

'Where are the others?' asked Signora Strega-Borgia. 'I'm starving, what's for tea? D'you know, Titus, I haven't eaten a decent chip since I left here last week. I could *die* for Mrs McLachlan's cooking.'

'I think it's Marie Bain's turn tonight,' said Titus, as they walked entwined towards the Schloss kitchen.

'Oh dear,' said Signora Strega-Borgia.

The smell that assaulted them from the open kitchen door could have been bottled and sold as an offensive weapon. Marie Bain hunched by the range, defensively stirring while Mrs McLachlan hovered nearby trying to be tactful.

'I don't think I've heard of that, dear,' she said. 'Don't you feel that three-quarters of an hour is a mite too long for a wee potato?'

Marie Bain sniffed in a disapproving way, and pointedly turned her back on the nanny.

'Heavens, dear, I didn't mean to criticize – I'm

sure you know better than I how to boil a tattie, and what *is* that delicious fish you're cooking?'

Marie Bain brightened slightly and lifted the lid on seven leathery haddocks. 'Ees smocked hiccup, the Signora's favoureet,' she said, prodding the pallid fish, as if to check that she had, indeed, succeeded in murdering them.

At the kitchen door, Signora Strega-Borgia looked at her son, put her finger to her lips and drew him back into the corridor. 'Shhh. Don't say a word. Just find Pandora and Damp, and tell them it's suppertime.'

'But I *hate* haddock and sprouts,' moaned Titus.

'Bring your sisters and I'll see you in the dining room in ten minutes.'

'I shan't eat it,' warned Titus, as his mother rolled up her sleeves and strode into the kitchen.

Marie Bain placed the last plateful in front of Damp. Damp took one look at what was in front of her and opened her mouth to howl.

'How *lovely*, Marie,' said Signora Strega-Borgia. She unfurled her napkin and tied it under Damp's chin. 'My favourite, smocked hiccup . . .'

'And ees also bottled sprats,' added the cook, helpfully identifying the pile of swamp greens attacking the hiccup.

'I'm sure we shall all dine like kings,' lied Signora Strega-Borgia. 'Thank you, Marie. Please don't wait up for us, we'll clear our own dishes tonight.'

Marie Bain, wreathed in smiles, departed for the kitchen, leaving Mrs McLachlan and the family to the privacy of the dining room.

'I'd rather starve than eat this,' said Pandora, glaring at her plate.

'I did try, dear,' said Mrs McLachlan, 'but Marie Bain is so sensitive to any criticism . . .'

'Tell me about it,' agreed Titus. 'If we leave anything on our plates, she'll go into a sulk for days.'

'I have a surprise for you all,' announced Signora Strega-Borgia, producing a slim metal rod from beneath the table. 'I learned some new spells at the Institute this week – nothing too adventurous, just level II Shrinking, advanced Enlarging and a smattering of Transformation.'

'You first, Titus,' she said, sliding his plate towards herself. Her wand described several circles around the plate, at first, slow and deliberate, and then as she gained confidence, faster and faster, until the tip of the wand became a blur of light. The unwanted plateful began to fade, as if all its colour was being drained away, until it looked like a black-and-white line drawing of a plate with blobs of food on it. The candles in the middle of the table flickered as Signora Strega-Borgia used her wand as an eraser, and bit by bit, rubbed out the inedible dinner.

'Wow!' gasped Pandora, looking meaningfully at her brother. 'I wish I could do that.'

'Mum, that's really cool, but . . .' said Titus.

'Ow!' yelled Signora Strega-Borgia, dropping the wand onto the tablecloth. 'The beastly thing keeps on overheating.' She plucked the wand from the smouldering tablecloth, and plunged it into a nearby wine bottle where it bubbled and spat for a moment before subsiding with a small eruption of steam. 'Pretty neat, huh?' she said, in triumph. 'Who's next?'

'Mum,' Titus clutched his stomach. 'I'm *starving*.'

'Ah,' said Signora Strega-Borgia, decanting the wand from the wine bottle. 'I'm not very adept at the next bit – we did do a spot of fizzy water into claret and princes into frogs stuff – let's see if I can remember . . .'

Mrs McLachlan and the family watched in amazement as Signora Strega-Borgia used her wand to draw lines of light on the tablecloth. The lines began to describe the shape of a large pudding-bowl full of something. Damp's eyes grew wide. Signora Strega-Borgia's wand was behaving like a paintbrush, filling colour in between the lines.

'Very nice, dear,' said Mrs McLachlan approvingly. 'Lemon meringue pie and mint ice cream, by the look of it?'

A puff of smoke came from the end of the wand, and with a small wheeze, it flopped, dangling from its owner's hand like a dead eel. 'Blast this thing,' muttered Signora Strega-Borgia, trying to make the wand stand up straight. The wand curled up like a pretzel and gave out a dying rattle.

Meanwhile Titus dug his spoon into his ice cream and scooped a huge spoonful into his mouth. 'Blaaark,' he spat. 'Brussels sprout ice cream!'

Damp's bottom lip popped out and began to quiver.

Titus approached the pie with extreme caution, dissecting a minute sliver, and gingerly placing it on his tongue.

'Well?' asked Pandora, enjoying the delightful spectacle of her brother gagging into his napkin. 'Do tell?'

Titus grabbed his water glass and rinsed his mouth thoroughly. 'Haddock and potato meringue pie,' he groaned.

Mrs McLachlan rose to her feet, piled up the unwanted plates and scraped the leftovers into an ornamental potpourri bowl.

'How are you going to hide that lot from Marie Bain?' asked Pandora.

Mrs McLachlan poked her head round the door to the hall and called 'Kno-ot . . . Ffu-u-up . . . Sab . . . Din-dins!'

The approaching thunder of yeti-pad, dragon-claw and gryphon-toe was punctuated by a crash and a crescendo of shrieks from Marie Bain.

'Coast's clear,' announced Mrs McLachlan, heading out the door with the bowl of leftovers. 'Anyone for chips?'

The Night
Outside . . .

Signora Strega-Borgia was walking the pets before bedtime. Tock waddled happily alongside his beloved mistress, Ffup and Sab flew overhead and Knot lagged behind, occasionally rolling in dirt and sniffing in puddles.

Signora Strega-Borgia swung their leashes and inhaled the night air. 'Just a bit further,' she said, 'and then we must go home to our beds . . . Sab and Ffup, you haven't gone yet, have you?'

Two spectacular crashes in the bushes, followed by a spreading smell informed her that the gryphon and the dragon had performed obediently.

'Good boys,' she said encouragingly. 'But, oh dear, those dinner leftovers didn't agree with you, did they?'

Knot belched loudly from behind a flowering

shrub. Its white flowers wilted slightly, and Tock stopped in his tracks, covered his nose with his paw and honked piteously.

In the distance an owl hooted. Knot listened intently and began to drool. 'Not now, Knot. You've *been* fed,' said Signora Strega-Borgia, stopping by the edge of the duck pond to shake a stone free of her shoe.

Tock sighed. It had been a few weeks since he'd sunk his teeth into a decent nanny, and although it was too dark to see the ducks, he could *smell* them. He opened his jaws with a creak and dipped an experimental claw into the water . . . Signora Strega-Borgia sneezed explosively. At once five startled ducks took flight and a lovelorn toad fell backwards off his lilypad and sank into the darkness of the pond. Tock closed his jaws with a disappointed honk.

'Blast it,' said Signora Strega-Borgia, sneezing again. Tock gazed at his mistress in alarm, as she rooted around in her pockets, hunting for something to wipe her nose with.

'Aaaachoo, not *again*. Oh, where are my tissues? Aaaachoo, oh *dear* . . . Knot? Knot, come here, pet.'

The yeti obediently shuffled closer until he stood beside Signora Strega-Borgia. She took one of his matted and hairy arms, brought it up to her face, and delicately wiped her nose with it.

'Better. Thanks Knot, but stay close till we're home, I might need you again. Aaachoo.' Sneezing fitfully, Signora Strega-Borgia headed for home. The StregaSchloss lay before her, tucked snugly into a fold of land that tapered off into the sea-loch. Faraway lights glimmered across the water. The distant puttering of a lobster boat putting out to sea and the leathery flap of Sab and Ffup wheeling around overhead were the only sounds disturbing the silence. StregaSchloss looked like a ship at sea.

Unfortunately, a captainless ship, thought Signora Strega-Borgia, blinking rapidly to forestall the inevitable tears that came when her thoughts turned to her missing husband. Captainless, but not adrift, she reminded herself. Sailing with Mrs McLachlan firmly at the helm. For the umpteenth time Signora Strega-Borgia gave silent thanks for the good fortune that had brought dear, sensible, Nanny McLachlan to StregaSchloss.

Her home beckoned, its dark mass dotted here and there with lights shining from windows, magically afloat in a night garden.

'Aaachoo,' sneezed Signora Strega-Borgia, breaking the spell.

Wordlessly, Knot extended an arm.

And the Night Within

I'm only doing this because I'm desperate, thought Pandora, tiptoeing into her mother's bedroom. The room was in darkness, but she could just about make out the shape of Signora Strega-Borgia's briefcase on top of her bed. I wouldn't do this normally, you understand, continued Pandora, undoing the buckles and pressing open the latch. Raising the lid, she opened the briefcase and gazed inside.

On first glance, the contents were disappointing. Ordinary, even. One half-eaten chicken sandwich plus crumpled biscuit wrapper, one pocket calculator, a small mobile phone, a packet of assorted wands (with seven left in the pack) and one A4 ring binder. What, no toads? thought Pandora. No vials and philtres? Not even a Collapsa-Cauldron or some dehydrated Eye V Newt? She picked out the packet of disposable wands and removed three to her pyjama pocket. In the darkness she failed to notice the small print on one wand that proclaimed it to be a: *Contrawand – undoes charms, reverses spells and nixes hexes*, and in even smaller print: *The manufacturers recommend six (6) uses only before disposal as hazardous magic waste.*

Intrigued by the ring binder, Pandora found it to be full of page upon page of her mother's handwriting. Hmm, thought Pandora, this looks promising . . . She meditatively ate the remainder of the chicken sandwich, reading by the dim light from the open doorway, and after a couple of pages, found what she was looking for. It read:

WK 4 Transthingummy, Shrinking and ~~Eggsdgeration Exxageration~~ Exaggerashun Experiment One — water into wine, princes into frogs etc.

Wand   ⟳ ×7   ⟲ ×9   ↝↟ ×1   ⟳ ×3

n.b. steady hand required

Downstairs, the front door opened and Pandora heard her mother's voice calling the pets to order. A honk and a splash from the moat signified Tock's bedtime and the sound of footfalls and rattling chains meant that Signora Strega-Borgia was leading Sab, Ffup and Knot back to the dungeon. That gave Pandora about two minutes to leave the bedroom exactly as she had found it.

Stuffing everything back into the briefcase, she carefully removed three relevant pages of spells from the ring binder, wedged them under her pyjama top and replaced the binder in the briefcase. She had just enough time to press the latch home, buckle the straps and hurl the briefcase back on the bed, before she heard her mother sneezing her way back up from the dungeon.

Pandora slipped away along the corridor and down one flight of steps to her own bedroom. Judging by the lack of light from under Titus's door, he had fallen asleep, happy in the knowledge that his sister was one day closer to her swim with Tock. 'Just you wait, Titus,' she muttered, pulling the quilt over her head and turning on her torch. 'First I'll get to grips with these wands, and then ... you're toast.' She removed the sheets of spells from under her pyjama top and began to commit them to memory.

The Schloss slept, the heavy air full of dreams, the gentle lapping of waves on the shore forming a tidal rhythm to doze by. Deep in her Polar night, Strega-Nonna dreamt of igloos and ice. Her freezer bed hummed and clicked, powered by a thin cable that snaked between the sleeper and the wall socket. The cable trailed across several yards of floor, dipping for half its length into a yellow puddle. This puddle consisted of fluids that had oozed out from Pandora's neglected pile of fish fingers, profiteroles and ice creams. At first it was a rather nasty combination of fish drip, chocolate and cream leak and banana, mint-chocolate-chip and strawberry ooze. That had been fourteen hours ago.

In the gentle warmth of the cellar, the puddle now could be safely described as a biological hazard. Bacteria formed, grew, reached adulthood, had babies and became grandparents. Teeming millions fed on the puddle, came back for second helpings, belched microscopically, and, due to the richness of the feast, passed large quantities of noxious gases. The puddle bubbled and heaved like a small swamp. The puddle stank. To Multitudina, who had missed bacon-rind breakfast, the puddle was the nearest thing to heaven that she'd ever smelled.

Oh YES, she thought, running at it at full tilt. Oh YES, oh YES, she continued, rolling up her top lip to expose her long yellow teeth. Mmmhmmm, sweet fishy rancidness, mmhmm, sour cheesy putrefaction, mmHMMM taste that decay, mmHmMM? rubbery chewiness? . . . BANG! uh oh . . . FLASSSSH.

Those fireworks were quite unnecessary, thought Multitudina, rubbing her burnt nose and assessing herself for whisker-loss. Good food doesn't need that kind of embellishment. Squeaking with outrage, she bolted out of the cellar and scuttled upstairs to her refuge under Titus's bed.

The freezer, in the silent way of such things, began to adapt to life as a large box. The thaw had begun.

Magic for Beginners

Morning dawned, wet and grey at StregaSchloss. Rain pitted the surface of the moat like a bad case of acne, and Tock sulked under a waterlily thicket. Puddles formed, gutters ran and windows misted up inside. The dungeons tended to seep and drip in bad weather, and out of pity, Mrs McLachlan had allowed Sab, Ffup and Knot into the kitchen to dry off. By the range, Marie Bain was stirring a pot of volcanic porridge, her yellow feet incongruously clad in fluffy pink slippers adorned with little bunnies. Mouth pursed and eyes grimly slitted she was trying to ignore Knot, who gazed fixedly at the cook's feet, and hoped against hope that she was wearing his breakfast.

Titus sat opposite the Beasts, sneezing occasionally

and steadily working his way through the healthy part of breakfast in the hope of reaching the unhealthy part before his jaws collapsed from exhaustion.

'More muesli, dear?'

'Nnnng,' he replied, chewing heroically.

When Mrs McLachlan turned her back on him to assess the status of her baking raspberry muffins, Titus slid his muesli bowl over to Ffup.

The dragon glared at him. 'Forget it, pal,' he hissed, pushing it back to Titus with a disdainful talon. 'After last night's offering, I'm *never* going to eat your leftovers again.'

Titus raised a hopeful eyebrow at Sab. The gryphon's eyeballs immediately turned to stone. Titus sighed. Knot was oblivious to everything but Marie Bain's feet, encased as they were in such delicious pink fluffiness . . . With another deep sigh, Titus began his fortieth spoonful of muesli.

Upstairs Pandora was examining the plunder from her mother's briefcase.

'With this kind of spell, I could shrink you as small as a bug,' muttered Pandora, conducting an imaginary conversation with her absent brother. 'And squash you so *flat* that your insides would come out with a splat . . .'

One and three-quarter Disposawands later, Pandora was getting the hang of magic. At first light, she'd crept out of bed, re-read the relevant instructions in the papers from the ring binder, and selected her first victim. Dangling from its hanger, adorned with layers of frills, lace and petticoats, was her most hated dress. Cause of many wardrobe wars, the dress had perversely survived each and every one of Pandora's attempts to destroy it. 'But *this* time . . .' she gloated, circling it with one of her purloined wands, '*this* time . . .'

The lace on the collar lifted and stirred in the breeze caused by Pandora's passes with the wand. With a tiny metal clatter it fell, complete with tiny metal hanger, onto the floor at her feet. Diminishing after-images faded in its wake – identical dresses for eight-, seven-, six-, five-, four-, three-, two-, Damp-year-olds, babies and newborns, each one smaller than the next, each one fading slowly away until, with a gasp, Pandora picked up the smallest version from the floor. 'When I find Multitudina's babies, this will be just *perfect* for one of them,' she said, holding the tiny thing in the palm of her hand.

Several hours later, Pandora's room had undergone a radical transformation. From the curtain poles hung two pocket-handkerchief-sized curtains. A miniature library of books the size of postage stamps huddled forlornly at the end of a large bookcase, lost in the vast space that now surrounded them. Pandora's wardrobe had become her new jewellery box and the bedroom floor was dotted with thumbnail-sized teddies and dolls. There had been a few casualties along the way –

where she was going to sleep might present a problem since her bed was now the size of a matchbox, and CDs the size of pinheads were frankly useless, but Pandora was feeling triumphant.

'Easy peasy, lemon squeezy,' she said. '*Now* for something trickier.' She flung herself onto her bed, forgetting that it had been an early casualty of the learning process. There was a tiny crunch from beneath her leg. 'First thing I'll try is matchsticks into mattresses,' she muttered, picking out the splinters.

A Little Family History

Luciano Strega-Borgia breakfasted alone. He sat flanked by coffee pots, little dishes of apricot jam, platters of prosciutto and enough croissants to feed a small army. However, the fact remained that his left ankle was chained to the table, and next to his plate was a document requiring his signature. Gazing out at the cypresses mirrored in the lake, he wondered if he'd ever see his wife and family again. His appetite deserted him as he remembered the morning he'd stormed out of StregaSchloss, all those weeks ago . . .

It had started with bickering at breakfast.

He'd come downstairs to the kitchen where his family were eating breakfast. The table was already awash with milk. Damp was grizzling and Titus and Pandora were looking particularly glum. At the head of the table, his

*wife of many years, the beautiful Signora Strega-Borgia,
sat with her head buried in the local paper. At the range,
wearing a particularly black scowl, Marie Bain stood
murdering a panful of scrambled eggs.*

*On seeing her father, Damp threw her hands in the air,
sending her cereal bowl skidding off the table and across
the floor. She bounced up and down in her clip-on baby
seat, causing everything on the table to bounce up and
down in tandem. Coffee and orange juice slopped out of
cups and glasses. Cereal packets toppled over and spilled
their contents.*

*Serenely unaware of the squalor surrounding her,
Signora Strega-Borgia stirred her coffee with the end of a
pencil, licked it dry and circled something in the paper.*

*Signor Strega-Borgia sat down at the breakfast table.
Damp hurled her cup at him by way of welcome. Marie
Bain placed a plate of blackened eggs in front of him.*

'Dad, I've got a bit of a problem,' said Titus.

'That's a major understatement,' said Pandora,
scattering sugar over her cereal, the surrounding tablecloth and, ultimately, the floor.

'Dad,' said Titus, ignoring his sister, 'you know you let
me load Death and Destruction II onto your computer?'

'Titus, you are terminally boring, d'you know that?'
interrupted Pandora. 'All you ever do is talk about computers from the moment you open your eyes in the
morning until . . .'

'Shut up, Pan,' said Titus. 'It's rude to interrupt.'

'It's even ruder to bore the pants off everyone,' mumbled
Pandora through a mouthful of Ricey Krispettes. Several

_____ 87

Ricey Krispettes were launched floorwards with each word.

Damp, her baby barometer sensing an impending storm, began to wail.

'Well, the problem is . . . Dad? Dad? Are you listening?'

'AAAARGH!' yelled Signor Strega-Borgia.

'Something wrong, darling?' said Signora Strega-Borgia, dropping her paper in the communal milk pool.

'TOO RIGHT, SOMETHING'S WRONG!' yelled Signor Strega-Borgia illogically.

Damp began to cry in earnest.

'Dad, look, I'm really sorry I crashed your computer, but it wasn't my fault,' blurted Titus.

Signor Strega-Borgia leapt to his feet, causing his chair to crash backwards onto the floor. 'I've had it!' he shouted at his family. 'I'm sick of living in a pigsty.' He waved at the table. 'I'm sick of eating pigswill.' He hurled his plate at the wall. 'And above all, I'm fed up to the back teeth with the lot of you.'

His family looked at him in dismay. In the background, Marie Bain curled up on the floor with the broken crockery and tried to make herself invisible. Above her head, scrambled eggs tracked slowly down the wall.

'Well . . .' said Signora Strega-Borgia icily, 'you know what you can do about that, don't you?'

'Mum . . .' warned Pandora.

'Dad?' pleaded Titus. 'Dad . . .'

'Mummy and Daddy need to have a little talk, darlings,' said Signora Strega-Borgia, in an icy voice. 'Why don't you all go upstairs while we sort ourselves out?' She fixed her children with a wide smile. Unfortunately, noted Titus, *it wasn't the kind of smile that reached her eyes.*

'Please *don't fall out?'* he begged.

'Please *go upstairs. Now. And take the baby,'* said Signora Strega-Borgia, standing up and opening the kitchen door.

In a hush full of unanswered questions, the children trooped out of the kitchen, followed by Marie Bain who dabbed at her eyes with her apron and sniffed disapprovingly. The sound of their footsteps died away, leaving Signor Strega-Borgia and his wife in silence.

A faraway clock chimed the hour.

'Well . . .' said Signora Strega-Borgia, sitting down and examining her fingernails.

'I'd best be off, then,' said her husband, hoping that he didn't have to go.

'As you wish,' said Signora Strega-Borgia, retrieving her newspaper from the milk pool. Her hands trembled and her eyes filled with tears, but she hid herself behind the soggy newsprint. It was this apparent lack of concern and frosty dismissal that made Signor Strega-Borgia's mind up.

'Don't expect me back for supper,' he said, glaring at her bent head. His words failed to penetrate her chilly armour. 'Or tomorrow,' he added, from the door.

'Bye,' said his wife, from behind the paper where her face was wet with tears. 'Lock the gate after you . . .'

With a massive attempt at injured dignity, Signor Strega-Borgia walked out on his life, his wife and his family. And from there on, it had all been downhill.

Somewhere along the road, he'd taken a wrong turn-

ing and he hardly recognized his surroundings. Moreover, by then it was way past lunchtime and he was starving. The shoulders of his jacket were soaked, his trousers were splattered with mud, and his stomach growled incessantly.

When the sleek black Mercedes pulled up beside him, his hair was plastered to his skull and he felt he'd sunk as low as it was possible to go. As the passenger door opened, he'd had no idea just how much further he still had to fall. . .

The sound of voices from outside the window dragged him back to the present. In the early morning Italian sunlight, Signor Strega-Borgia saw Pronto loading a violin case into the boot of a large black car.

'Don't worry, Maestro,' Pronto called to someone outwith the field of Signor Strega-Borgia's vision. 'It's time for them to face the music. When I finish, there won't be a single one left standing.'

Signor Strega-Borgia puzzled over this statement as he helped himself to another cup of coffee. Was Pronto such a talented musician that his performances literally brought the house down? Or was it that his skill with a violin was such that his concert audiences knelt before him in adoration?

Drawing a finger slowly across his throat, Pronto climbed into the rear seat, and the car drew away, its tyres crunching gravel and its black windows throwing back a reflection of the blank face of the Palazzo. In one of those moments where pennies drop and realization dawns, Signor Strega-Borgia twigged. Maybe it was nothing to do with music, he realized, as his legs turned to water and his heart leapt free of its moorings and flew into his mouth, maybe Pronto was on a deadly mission? To StregaSchloss!

Hearing the front door slam and the heavy tread of approaching footsteps, Signor Strega-Borgia drained his coffee cup and picked up the document that lay beside his untouched breakfast. It appeared to be a will. In fact, it appeared to be *his* will. Hardly believing the evidence of his eyes, Signor Strega-Borgia read that as the trustee for his son Titus, he had decided to make a few changes . . . Clutching his throat, Signor Strega-Borgia scanned the document:

After much thought . . . due to the corrupting influence of vast sums of money . . . Titus too young to inherit . . . I, Luciano Strega-Borgia, being of sound mind . . . hereby decree . . . in the event of my death . . . going to leave everything I possess to . . .

'NEVER!' he shouted, just as Don Lucifer's hairy nostrils appeared, as was their habit, three seconds before the rest of his half-brother.

'Never?' queried Don Lucifer, idly tapping the business end of a rather wicked-looking handgun.

'Um, yes, um, I was just saying I've never drunk

a finer cup of . . . um ah . . .' Luciano's words trailed off into silence.

The brothers' eyes met over the handgun. 'When you've signed that thing,' Don Lucifer remarked in a very matter-of-fact way, 'I need you to have a look at my computer. It's got some kind of virus playing havoc with the mainframe.'

'Lucifer, d'you think I'm a complete pushover? A total jelly that you can just shove around?'

Don Lucifer gazed impassively at his sibling. 'Yup,' he said, clicking the gun's safety catch to the off position, struck by the happy thought that the inhabitants of StregaSchloss would soon be dead, no matter what his jelly of a half-brother did. 'Don't be a fool, Luciano. Sign on the dotted line and then get downstairs and sort out my computer problem or, later on today, your precious son will have an unfortunate accident, resulting in his untimely demise. Guaranteed. So do as you're told, and don't waste any more of my time.'

It's only money, Signor Strega-Borgia told himself, as he signed away his stamp collection, his bank balance, Titus's inheritance and most importantly, StregaSchloss, his home. The thought of its acute vulnerability to invasion by Mafia thugs caused him to wish he'd installed a slightly more high-tech security system than a dungeonful of mythical beasts.

A vision of his beloved family under threat from a violin-bearing Italian menace caused him to burst into tears. 'Don't hurt them, Lucifer ... PLEASE? I'll do anything, but just leave my family out of this, I beg you, pleeeeease ...' He fell sobbing to the carpet, in the knowledge that he was, indeed, a jelly.

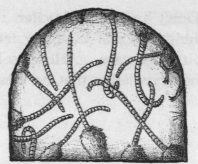

E-rats Redux

Luciano Strega-Borgia hobbled along the deserted corridors of the Palazzo, held at gunpoint by his brother, dimly aware that the floor had been newly polished with something that smelled vaguely of petrol. Indeed the marble floors shone so much that they were slightly slippery underfoot. Don Lucifer stopped at a little door marked TUG and pushed. Not surprisingly, nothing happened. Don Lucifer clapped himself on the forehead, tugged and entered.

Despite a total lack of human presence, the room seemed alive. Screens flickered, modems hummed and shrieked their strange peacock call and the noise of spinning disks and coolant fans merged with excited squeakings and scrapings coming from one corner of the room.

'It's all yours.' The Don indicated the room at large, and then grabbed Signor Strega-Borgia by the lapels. 'And don't be so stupid as to try and get help. You e-mail the Carabinieri, the FBI, the CIA, the Gendarmes, any form of police you like, and all the computers will crash instantly. It's been programmed to alert me if anyone keys in as much as 999. So don't even *think* about it. No calling for help, or you're fish food.' He released his quaking half-brother and smiled encouragingly. 'The virus. The rats. That's what you're here for. Get it sorted, Luciano, there's a good boy.' With this, Don Lucifer turned on his heels and walked out of the room, pushing the door shut behind him.

In a dazed state of obedience, Signor Strega-Borgia sought the source of the squeaking. Pulling up a chair, he sat in front of one screen that appeared to be running a most unusual screensaver. He looked more closely. That wasn't a screensaver. That was an infestation. Thirteen rat babies looked back at him through the glass. Beside them, a modem lit up and quietly exploded. The screen turned black and smoke began to leak apologetically from its rear.

'We have a problem,' muttered Signor Strega-Borgia, turning to a fresh screen and keying in a set of commands.

>YOU'RE ABSOLUTELY RIGHT, LAMEBRAIN> agreed the computer.

/QUERY SOURCE/ typed Signor Strega-Borgia, ignoring the insult.

>THAT'S FOR ME TO KNOW, AND YOU TO FIND OUT> said the computer, aggravating things further by adding ten rows of asterisks, this being a computer's equivalent of sticking its tongue out and yelling, 'Nya Nya, nah NYA NYA.'

'So, you don't wish to reveal your source, do you?' muttered Signor Strega-Borgia, and pressed five keys simultaneously.

Immediately the screen went black, and almost immediately, lit back up again. >NO NEED TO BE QUITE SO BRUTAL> complained the computer, >VIOLENCE NEVER SOLVED ANYTHING>

'No,' agreed Signor Strega-Borgia, 'but a quick crash and reboot might bring you to your senses.'

He typed /QUERY SOURCE/ again.

The computer replied with the equivalent of 'Wild Horses Wouldn't Drag That Information From Me': >MMMMMMMMMMM> it said.

Signor Strega-Borgia typed /REBOOT? QUERY?/

>MMMMNYA POO> replied the computer, adding, >I'LL NEVER REVEAL MY SOURCES, NO MATTER WHAT. MMMMMMM>

Signor Strega-Borgia resorted to desperate measures. Opening a bottle of brown fizzy liquid abandoned by a previous operator, he held it over the air vents on the computer.

/RIGHT/ he typed. /COKE IN THE VENTS OR — SOURCE. QUERY?/

>YOU NASTY BIG LAMEBRAINED BRUTE> complained the computer. >MAY YOUR HARD DISK CEASE TO SPIN, AND ALL YOUR FILES RASP. MAY ALL YOUR CRASHES BE FATAL AND YOUR REBOOTS BE DOC MARTENS . . .>

/SOURCE. QUERY? OR ELSE/ typed Signor Strega-Borgia.

>OH VERY WELL, BRAWN OVER BRAIN. STREGA-SCHLOSS.CO.UK. HAPPY NOW?>

'WHAT?' screamed Signor Strega-Borgia.

The computer, not possessing a pair of ears, didn't respond.

/QUERY. ERROR, SURELY?/ typed Signor Strega-Borgia, his hands suddenly clammy on the keyboard.

>NOPE NEGATIVE NIX NOT! STREGASCHLOSS.CO.UK IT IS. MMMMMMMM> replied the computer, adding two rows of ampersands by way of salt in the wound.

'Titus,' groaned Signor Strega-Borgia, slumping onto the keyboard. 'What have you *done*?'

How had his only son sent an infestation of rats across the ethernet and straight into his half-brother's unbelievably complex computer system? And, never mind how or even why, judging by Don Lucifer's threats, Titus could be in extreme danger. Feverishly, his fingers flying over the keys, Signor Strega-Borgia typed out a message.

titus@stregaschloss.co.uk

titus

something very wicked is about to arrive on your doorstep. don't ask. just do what i say.

try and get your mum and your sisters down into the dungeon with the beasts, and stay there until . . .

What? Until what? Until he got home? That was becoming more unlikely by the minute. Signor Strega-Borgia wasn't coming home, not if his evil half-brother had anything to do with it. He began again.

titus@stregaschloss.co.uk

titus

i've been kidnapped by a psychopathic relative. don't worry.

On reflection, he removed the last bit.

titus

i've been kidnapped and can't get home. i think you're all in grave danger as well. the best thing to do is panic.

This wasn't going at all well. He considered getting Titus to phone the police, but he knew that a twelve-year-old trying to tell the local Highland constabulary that he'd just had an e-mail from his estranged father saying that there was an unspecified threat on its way from somewhere unknown was *not* going to bring several officers in blue to the door of StregaSchloss. Plus, as his half-brother had been at such pains to point out, if he so much as typed 999, or 'police', the computer would alert Lucifer before it crashed . . . Think, man, he beseeched himself. Ah there it was, the kind of message that would convey the gravity of the situation in a fashion that his son might understand.

titus

aliens abducted me on my way to auchen-lochtermuchty, and are about to launch an attack on stregaschloss. i would have come home sooner but you know how uncool these beings with green aerials coming out of their foreheads can be.

take the beasts and your sisters and your mum and get as far away from stregaschloss as possible. please. please?

and be warned. the aliens will probably be armed and are definitely dangerous. be careful.

i love you

dad

p.s. did you send thirteen rats down the modem?

Signor Strega-Borgia keyed in a row of Xs and sat back, trembling. On-screen a dialogue box appeared: SEND?

Signor Strega-Borgia hit the ENTER key with such force that the plastic cracked and it divided in two, becoming the ENT and ER keys. On-screen the dialogue box read: MESSAGE SENT (BUT YOU DIDN'T HAVE TO BE QUITE SO NEANDERTHAL).

Signor Strega-Borgia ignored this and began to chew his fingernails. On a nearby screen, twenty-six rat eyes glared pinkly out at him. They were assessing his food value (minimal), his general value to ratkind (zilch) and his intelligence (non-existent since he hadn't brought any bacon rinds). Bored, the rats turned away and began to gnaw pixels by the dozen.

Damp on the Web

Mrs McLachlan's raspberry muffins were good, thought Titus, rather too good, in fact. After eating more than his fair share (eight out of twelve) he headed upstairs to his computer. When the screen flickered into life, a dialogue box appeared with: YOU HAVE MAIL on it.

'Spam,' muttered Titus under his breath, ignoring the announcement, and loading *Death & Destruction II* into the CD-ROM.

The dialogue box politely made itself scarce, waiting until Titus had assembled his armies onscreen, equipped them with a bristling array of weaponry and was just about to begin the assault on the peaceful kingdom of computer-generated Nettlefold. Titus paused, fingers hovering above the keyboard. There was that annoying dialogue box getting in the way again. All unknowing, the innocent citizens of the kingdom of Nettlefold slept on into oblivion. They remained unaware that the agent of their destruction was a large box hanging in the sky that bore the legend:

YOU STILL HAVE MAIL. THE KIND OF MAIL THAT DOESN'T LIE MEEKLY ON THE MAT WAITING TO BE OPENED. THIS IS MAIL WITH MENACES. IT DEMANDS TO BE READ, OR ELSE . . .

Titus groaned. Not again. *Death & Destruction II* was always pulling this kind of stunt. The trouble was that it was such an aggressive game. Every time he loaded it, it tried to pick a fight with everything in its way – first the CD-ROM, then the RAM, then the processor. Maybe he'd try it again, later. In the meantime, out with *Death & Destruction II* and check the mailbox.

Titus sat back and waited. The dialogue box disappeared again, muttering darkly to itself. After a lot of whirring fans and little clicky noises from deep within the computer, a message appeared onscreen.

UNLESS YOU OPEN YOUR MAIL NOW THIS COMPUTER WILL TURN INTO A LARGE WHITE BOX THAT HAS NO MEMORY OF BEING ANYTHING OTHER THAN A LARGE WHITE BOX.

'OK, OK. Chill *out* would you?' groaned Titus, pressing ENTER. His eyes grew wide. 'WHAT?' he yelled. 'Dad? What is this rubbish?'

His fingers a blur on the keyboard, Titus replied:

dad@mafia.org.ital
for signor strega-borgia, missing father of titus, abandoner of family etc.
dear sir
the rats belong to your daughter. perhaps you'd like to ask HER how they got there? anyway, aliens don't have aerials coming out of their heads. that's SAD, dad. think of a better excuse. and none of this is my fault.
hope you're well,
your son, titus

He pressed ENTER, wiped a tear off the keyboard and reloaded *Death & Destruction II*. Nettlefold didn't stand a chance.

Signor Strega-Borgia burst into dramatic tears when Titus's message arrived on-screen. Immediately, he responded:

titus@stregaschloss.co.uk
for titus strega-borgia's eyes only. master of the mouse, genius of the joystick, beloved only son of luciano the low, dad the sad.
my dear titus,

pax?

please forgive me – the alien idea was pretty sad, i admit. however, it's not an excuse. i was kidnapped, but by some rather scary gangsters, not aliens, and i'm stuck in a dungeon somewhere in the italian countryside. titus, i can't get home just yet. i'm not sure, but i think one of the gangsters may be on his way to stregaschloss. just in case, could you lock all the doors and somehow keep your mother and sisters (and yourself, of course!) in the same room as ffup, knot and sab. and tock too, if you can manage.

and stay away from the windows.

call me a paranoid old dad, but until i'm back home to look after you all myself, do me a favour and humour your ancient father, huh? i miss you every day, and love you lots.

hugs and more hugs, dad.

p.s. have you worked out how to trash nettlefold yet?

There ... done. He'd struck the right balance between giving a clear warning and not throwing Titus into a terror-stricken panic. And he hadn't once mentioned police, so his message wouldn't alert Lucifer's alarm system. Feeling faintly smug, Signor Strega-Borgia carefully pressed ENT and ER simultaneously, and sent his message winging out across the Web. He sat back in his chair, wiping his streaming face with his sleeve. For some reason, the air-conditioning in the computer room appeared to be malfunctioning, but thankfully the pervasive smell of petrol-based floor polish had gone.

Above the smoking remains of Nettlefold a giant box hung in the sky.

Titus sniffed as he typed in a message:

dad@mafia.org.ital

dear dad

yeah, right, dad. so it's gangsters now, not aliens with aerials? have the gangsters got machine guns in violin cases as well? ha ha.

get a life, dad. i'm 12 not 2. and if you think i'm letting sab, tock, ffup and knot into my bedroom, you can think again. they're not toilet-trained yet. hurry up and come home. we all miss you.

lots of love

titus

p.s. nettlefold is toast

It was at this tender moment that Pandora threw open the door to her brother's bedroom, and announced that Titus, too, was going the same way as the computer-generated kingdom of Nettlefold.

'Titus, you're toast. You're history. You're about to be an ex-Titus . . .' she gloated, waving a disposable wand for emphasis.

'Go *away* Pandora,' muttered Titus, his eyes not leaving the screen, 'I know where your rats went, and believe me, they're *not* coming back.'

Wearing a brand new nappy, and modelling a

dazzlingly pink pair of dungarees, Damp crawled into Titus's bedroom to check if the face was still hungry. Titus and Pandora were too engrossed in mutual slander to notice her crawling purposefully towards the computer. Damp gazed upwards at the CD-ROM drawer in adoration. With an inaudible shriek from the hard disk, *Death & Destruction II* crashed again, causing the CD drawer to spring open and eject the quarrelsome disk. Damp crawled closer for a good look. At this point, time appeared to speed up and everything began to happen rather quickly.

Upon hearing the CD-ROM drawer open, and curious as to whether the bacon rinds were still inside, Multitudina made a run for the computer. Behind Titus's back, Pandora began to draw circles with her wand. Faster and faster until, just before the final thrust, she stepped forward, tripped over the running Multitudina and aimed her final blast not at Titus, but at Damp.

Titus, fingers poised over the keyboard, about to send his letter to dad@mafia.org.ital, gave an enormous sneeze that launched his miniaturized baby sister into orbit. Currently about the size of a small thumbnail, Damp was blown into the open CD drawer, and spun upwards into the modem.

As the sneeze left Titus's nose, his fingers reflexively pressed ENTER. On-screen a dialogue box informed him: MESSAGES SENT. It was Pandora's terrible scream that told him what he had really sent.

Pronto Gets Help

Flying from Italian sunshine into Scottish drizzle had done nothing to improve Pronto's mood. Dressed for a kinder climate, he was soaked to the skin by the time he arrived at the dingy dockside offices of the Edinburgh branch of Rent-a-Thug. His shoes squelched, his suit dripped black dye and his mobile phone was suspiciously soggy. Across the desk from him, a fat man in a pin-stripe suit rolled his eyes heavenwards, and wheezed into a telephone receiver buried under his many chins. 'Danny the Fox is doing a six-to-ten stretch, huh? What about Sid the Slash?'

A polite knock at the door, and the fat man's secretary poked her head round. 'There's a Mr Machiavelli from Garrottes R Us in reception for you, boss,' she trilled.

The fat man gave her the thumbs up sign.

'And that consignment of Uzi nine millimetres has just arrived – shall I unpack them now?'

The fat man nodded, and waved her away with an impatient hand. 'Too bad,' he murmured down the telephone. 'He should have stuck to his knives, our Sid. Semtex is such unforgiving stuff . . .' He paused and scratched his armpit in a thoughtful kind of way. 'So, what can you do for me? What've you got left? Yeah, I need one more for this very special client.' He grinned an unpleasant gold-capped grin across the desk at Pronto. 'Yeah, the usual arrangement, yeah, that's right. Half up front, the remainder when the job's done. So . . . who have you come up with? Attila? Attila what? What sort of a name is that? Hang on, I'll ask my client.'

The fat man gagged the telephone with one vast paw, and leant across the desk to Pronto. 'My friend says he's got a real nutter for you. Guy by the name of Attila the Bun.'

Pronto raised one eyebrow.

'Yeah, I know, but it gets better. Apparently he wears a full rabbit suit all the time – hence the nick-name, but my friend says he's one of the best in the business.'

Pronto raked the fat man with a disbelieving stare.

The fat man oozed back across the desk and slumped in his chair. 'Look, pal, you can take it or leave it. S'up to you. All I know is you want four professional personnel-terminators for a job up in the Highlands, no questions asked, *and* you want them *now*, a.s.a.p., pronto, toot sweet . . .'

'How did you get my name?' interrupted Pronto.

'Look, Toots, or whatever you call yourself, get this – I can't find you four expert terminators at such short notice. Three I can do, four, no can do. Either you take this Tillybun bloke and we've got a deal, or you're stuck with the three we got.'

Pronto decided.

'Right, squire, we've got a deal,' said the fat man, retrieving the receiver from his clammy fist and replacing it under his chins. 'OK, we cut the rabbit in. Usual place, give my client an hour to find himself a motor. Yeah, yeah, he knows the form. Used notes, in the left luggage at the station. Yeah. You too. Bye.' Sweating copiously, the fat man replaced the receiver and collapsed in his chair. Mopping his face with a lace-trimmed handkerchief, he began to draw a map for Pronto.

Exactly one hour later, Pronto arrived in a hired van at the agreed rendezvous. Edinburgh was in the grip of Festival fever, and the chosen location was thronged with tourists, street performers, jugglers, acrobats and, regrettably, more than one fully dressed rabbit.

Pronto had no trouble spotting his three experts. They stood in a group, wearing sunglasses, black suits and deep scowls. They were far more conspicuous in the crowd of brightly dressed, happy Festival-goers than their companion in his rabbit costume. As instructed by the fat man, Pronto stuck his head out of the van window, pretending to ask directions from passers-by. 'Anyone know where I can find a theatre group called Terminator Four?' he yelled.

Three large guys began to move in his direction. Nearby, a well-dressed rabbit detached himself from an audience of small children, and began to hop towards the van. One small boy appeared to be reluctant to say goodbye. He clung determinedly to the rabbit's leg, his face crumpling with the effort.

The three large men climbed into the rear of the van, holding the door open for their lopsidedly hopping companion.

'Ger OFF,' the rabbit growled at the limpet-like child. 'Leggo, or I'll . . .'

Abruptly, the child let go before he could complete his threat. The rabbit bounded into the back of the van, slamming the door behind him.

Across the street, an apprentice piper, in full highland dress, began to coax the opening bars of *Auld Lang Syne* from his bagpipes. It sounded awful, but it masked the squeal of brakes and the child's earsplitting wail, 'That bunny's got a GUN!'

Swerving to overtake a caravan, Pronto shuddered at the memory. In the passenger seat beside him, the rabbit twiddled dials on the radio, played with the heater controls and wound the window up and down, all the while keeping up an endless flow of chatter.

'Know what this motor needs, eh?' he asked of the company in general. 'Needs some of them furry dice, dunnit?' he said to no-one in particular. 'My mate's motor, now there's a really cool set of wheels – he's got the dice, tinted windows, alloy wheels, sound system big enough ter blow the windows out . . .'

'How useful,' muttered Pronto. 'No vehicle should be without one.'

'That's what I mean,' continued the rabbit. 'And he's got satellite navigation, turbo-charged twin-cam fuel-injected whatchamacallits . . .'

'*Really?*' said Pronto, investing that one word with every ounce of sarcasm at his disposal. 'And your "friend", what does he do?'

'Eh? What d'you mean, "what does he do"?'

'I mean,' said Pronto, speaking very slowly and carefully. 'What. Does. He. Do. For. A. Living. Your. Friend.?'

'Uhh. I get your meaning. He doesn't do nothing for a living. He's dead.'

'Oh dear, how sad,' said Pronto insincerely.

The van began to slow down as they approached a vast rusting bridge. Pronto raked through his pockets, and turned round in his seat. 'Look, we have to pay to cross this toll bridge. Has anyone got any change? I only have big notes.'

'I haven't any pockets, pal,' said the rabbit, stating the obvious.

Mutters from the rear of the van told Pronto that, like him, everyone was carrying either credit cards or rolls of big notes.

'Couldn't we just drive straight through the barrier?' said the rabbit hopefully.

'No, we could *not*,' growled Pronto. 'We are trying not to draw any attention to ourselves. Here we are on a clandestine mission to some Highland fortress, intent on rubbing out a boy and anyone else that sees us do it. If we crash through the barrier, chances are we'll arrive at our destination with a police escort.'

The van rolled to a halt in front of the toll barrier. Pronto wound down his window and extended his arm with a £100 note at the end of it.

'Haven't you got anything smaller?' the toll collector asked in disgust, 'I haven't got change for *that*.'

'Tell him to keep the change,' said the rabbit, 'and hurry it up, will ya? I need the bog.'

'Will you shut *up* and let me deal with this,' hissed Pronto. 'He's hardly likely to forget several men and a rabbit who told him to keep £99.20 change, is he?'

'I can't wait much longer,' moaned the rabbit to himself, 'you've no idea how long it takes to get this rabbit costume undone . . . I'm gonna burst.'

A line of bridge traffic began to form behind the van. The toll collector stuck his head round the door of his booth, the better to address them. 'You'll just have to wait,' he yelled. 'Daddy Warbucks here hasn't anything smaller than a hundred-pound note, and I'll have to get some more change.' Grumbling to himself, he strolled slowly off in the direction of the other tollbooths, holding the bank-note out in front of him, as if it was covered in plague bacteria.

Minutes dragged past. By now, the rabbit was jiggling frantically on his seat, causing the entire van to bounce up and down. 'Oh oh oh. My bladder can't cope. I need a pee NOW – ow ow ow, it's like trying to stop Niagara Falls . . . urrrgh . . . hurry up, hurry up, hurry up.'

The toll collector was deep in conversation at a faraway booth where his ancient colleague was slowly counting out £99.20 in pennies. From time to time they glanced leisurely over to where the van was rocking back and forth, muffled screams coming from its interior.

To the amusement of the occupants in the long line of waiting cars, the van at the head of the queue suddenly stopped bouncing and ejected one of its passengers. What was going on? The ejectee appeared to be attempting to divest himself of a large rabbit suit. He appeared to be in something of a tearing hurry. No? No. The rabbit had changed his mind.

The rabbit was now waddling back to the van, his furry legs held apart, leaving a trail of wet rabbit footprints on the tarmac behind him.

The toll collector shuffled back to his booth, effortfully dragging a large canvas bag in which clinked £99.20 in coins. He stuck his head into the van, recoiled abruptly, and said, 'Phhwoah. What's that *smell*? Did someone die in there, while I was off getting your money?' He roared with laughter at his own wit, and began to count out Pronto's change.

Several miles up the road, they stopped at a service station and bought four cans of air freshener. Several miles after that, they stopped in a layby and sprayed the rabbit. Shortly thereafter, the roads narrowed considerably. A series of s-bends and steep dips conspired to make everyone feel very queasy indeed. Everyone, that is, except the rabbit. He was quite happy; his costume had dried off nicely, he'd found an excellent heavy metal station on the radio, and was rolling the window up and down in time to the beat.

'OPEN THE WINDAE!' yelled the three men in the back, as the van lurched and rolled around another corner.

Several miles later, they stopped in the middle of nowhere and tied the rabbit to the roof rack.

A Wee Hot Toddy

With the feeling that she might have lost several brownie points by tripping up her owner, Multitudina sneaked downstairs, back to the cellar. The smell of defrosted and rotting food had grown stronger since her last visit. A reeking lagoon surrounded the once-glacial freezer. I'm not tempted, Multitudina told herself firmly. Last time I sipped at *that* particular watering hole, my nose got fried. She gave the lake a wide berth, and continued on her travels. Somewhere in this huge house, she thought, her stomach growling, there must be something for a mother-to-be to eat.

The rain had finally stopped, and weak sunshine trickled in through the kitchen windows. Mrs

McLachlan glared at Sab, Ffup and Knot who huddled round the kitchen table.

'There were *four* left,' she said, tapping the muffin tray for emphasis, 'and now there are none.'

The beasts sighed sympathetically.

'I turned my back on them for one minute,' she continued, 'one minute while I heated up a wee hot toddy for the Signora, and when I turned round . . .'

Sab licked his lips nervously. Ffup stifled a belch with one leathery wing. Mrs McLachlan stared at them. Knot lolloped out of the kitchen, leaving a half-eaten bunny slipper on the chair behind him.

'Did he do it?' demanded Mrs McLachlan. 'All *four* raspberry muffins? What a *pig*. After that enormous dinner he ate last night.'

'Blaark,' said Sab, holding his feathery stomach.

'Don't feel well,' groaned Ffup, clutching his scaly one.

Mrs McLachlan opened the door to the kitchen garden. 'Not on the *herbs*,' she warned, as Sab and Ffup bolted past her. 'Oh well . . . never mind, they'll wash.'

Five minutes later, they returned, both looking rather pale and ill. 'Must have been the smocked hiccup,' whispered Ffup, wincing at the memory.

'Now I know why they're called Brussels Splats,' added Sab darkly.

Signora Strega-Borgia huddled under her bedcovers, a trail of tissues leading from the bathroom to her pillow. A fit of sneezing had left her as limp as an overcooked haddock, her throat felt as if she'd eaten a bowl of razor blades, and her nose ran like an Olympic athlete.

There was a discreet tap at the bedroom door, and Mrs McLachlan breezed in, bearing a little tray on which something steamed. 'Good morning, dear,' she said, setting the tray down on a squelching pile of used tissues. 'I've brought you a Morangie-Fiddach-Macallan special. Three spoonfuls of heather honey, the juice of a lemon, both warmed together with three cloves, a cinnamon stick and a blade of mace . . . oh, and did I mention? Three glasses of the finest whisky.'

She watched in approval as Signora Strega-Borgia drained the mug in several swallows. 'Nnngg,' said Signora Strega-Borgia, as her eyes crossed and perspiration broke out on her forehead.

Mrs McLachlan plumped pillows, smoothed the quilt, and tucked her employer in. 'S'got,' slurred Signora Strega-Borgia, flapping a hand at the empty mug, 's'got a kick like a mule . . . jusht closhe m'eyes forra bit . . .' She slumped deeper into the pillows and began to snore.

Mrs McLachlan drew the curtains shut, piled the tray with soggy tissues, and tiptoed out of the room. 'Is the wee one with you, Titus?' she called, heading downstairs.

Titus opened his bedroom door just enough to poke his head round. 'She's playing in the computer,' he said, truthfully.

Satisfied, Mrs McLachlan descended to the kitchen.

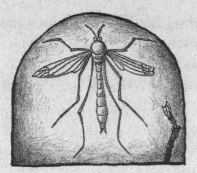

Arachnids with Attitude

Titus closed his bedroom door and turned the key in the lock. Across the room, Pandora chewed her fingernails and stifled a sob.

'What are we going to do, Titus? How do we get Damp back?'

'We can't,' Titus said, baldly.

'We *must* be able to,' wailed Pandora.

'It's like posting a letter,' explained Titus. 'Once you've *sent* something, you can't stick your hand into a post-box and pull it back out . . .'

'You can wait till the postman unlocks the post-box, and ask him to fish your letter out . . .'

'It's not the same thing,' said Titus, running his hands through his hair. 'We have to find out where she's gone, what address she's gone to, and then ask them to send her back.'

'We're talking about her as if she's a parcel,' sobbed Pandora. 'She's a *baby*.'

'She's a *lost* baby,' said Titus. 'And we have to find her before someone else does.'

'What d'you mean *we*?' said Pandora, in between mouthfuls of fingernails. 'I don't know anything about computers or the Internet.'

They gazed at the screen, each lost in their own thoughts. 'Neither do I, really,' admitted Titus. 'The Internet's like a big web, Pandora. It's absolutely vast. Colossal. Humungous. And somewhere, out there, on one of the millions of strands, is our baby sister.'

Pandora groaned and rolled back on Titus's bed. She stared at the ceiling, tears rolling down her face, aware of what little hope they had of retrieving Damp. 'Poor baby,' she wept. 'Lost on the Web. Stuck, like a . . . a fly, waiting helplessly for . . .'

'You called?' said a voice. Spinning down from the ceiling came a vast hairy spider.

Titus leapt backwards as Tarantella touched down on his monitor. She paused, flexing all eight of her furry legs, and smiling at him with her aggressively pink lips. 'YEEEEUCHH,' he said, flapping her away. 'Is she *still* alive? I thought I'd killed her years ago.'

Tarantella hip-hopped closer, stopping to cup her chin in one of her legs and gaze at this impudent human. 'What's his problem?' she asked Pandora.

'He's got several,' said Pandora. 'But mainly, he's got a thing about spiders.'

'AAARGH – a *talking* spider,' squeaked Titus. 'When did it learn to speak? And wear *lipstick*? EURCHH. Gross. Kill it, Pandora.' He climbed onto a chair and curled himself up into a spider-proof ball.

'Titus. Chill out. She's only a spider,' sighed Pandora.

'AAARGH – a talking *child*,' mocked Tarantella. 'Yeurk. Urg. Disgusting. And it's a *male* one too . . . kill it, Pandora.'

'Tarantella. Titus,' said Pandora, introducing one to the other. 'Do shut up, both of you. Listen, this is *really* important. We need you, Tarantella. Yes, *we*,' she added, quelling Titus with a glare. 'Tarantella knows about webs, you know about computers. Together you might be able to find Damp.'

'Is Damp the small wet thing that wears a toilet round her middle?' asked Tarantella, scuttling up a chair leg to face Pandora.

'Yes. Our four-legged baby sister,' said Pandora. 'She's lost on the biggest web ever.'

'How big?' said Tarantella, producing a tiny lipstick and applying it to her mouthparts.

'Urrgh. Aaak. Lipstick . . .' gagged Titus.

'Shut *up*, Titus,' said Pandora. 'The biggest ever,'

she continued to the spider, 'stretching all the way round the world, and back.'

'Lots of flies,' murmured Tarantella, licking her lips.

'More than you could eat in a lifetime,' said Pandora, adding, 'and ... it's all Multitudina's fault.'

'That verminous baggage,' spat Tarantella. 'High time she donated her miserable carcass to medical science.'

'We're straying off the point, Pan,' warned Titus. 'Time's flying and here you are rubbishing rodents while Damp wanders the Web.'

'You don't mind if I wrap her, before I bring her back?' said Tarantella, sidling towards the modem.

'Just don't accidentally eat her on the way home,' said Pandora, beginning to spin her Disposawand.

Titus instantly turned pale.

'What a revolting idea,' Tarantella rolled her eyes in disgust. 'Have you any idea how putrid human beings taste?' Her voice diminished as her tennis ball body shrank to the size of a full stop. Spitting delicately on the keyboard, she sprang into the air, and vanished into the open drawer of the CD-ROM. Her disembodied voice filtered out. 'Not a patch on a nice plump bluebottle ... or a sun-dried daddy-long-legs ... mmm ... deeeli-cious. So thoughtful of you to leave one in here for me ...' There was a tiny crunch as Tarantella bit into a mummified fly wing she'd discovered in a corner of the modem.

In a dreamy state of revolted fascination, Titus pressed ENTER.

A Warm Welcome

An ornately carved metal gate barred the road to StregaSchloss. It bore a sign that read:

WARNING
Trespassers will be
a. served for breakfast
b. turned into frogs
c. forced to eat Brussels sprouts

Scowling, Pronto braked hard, threw the van into reverse and backed down the road till he came to a patch of level ground shaded by some dusty chestnut trees. 'From now on, we go on foot,' he said, climbing down from the driver's seat and slouching to the rear of the van to unlock the back doors.

The three men in black unfolded their stiff legs and climbed out. Pronto retrieved his violin case from a rack inside the van and undid its clasps. Inside, nestled cosily on golden plush, lay a small machine gun. Pronto removed this, ripping away the plush to reveal several magazines of bullets. Threading these into the rapid load cartridge, he made several clicks and snaps of a sort commonly associated with Being Up To No Good.

From the roof of the van, a muffled moan reminded him of his forgotten colleague. 'Release the rabbit, would you?' he muttered to one of the men in black.

The man obeyed promptly, cutting the rabbit free with a wicked looking knife. The rabbit slid off the roof, and began to complain.

'You could have killed me with that stunt, you know,' he moaned. 'What if I'd fallen off?'

'Listen, Bun,' hissed the knife-wielder, 'one more peep out of you and you'll find yourself in pieces, shrink-wrapped in little polystyrene trays in the refrigerated section of your local supermarket. Do I make myself clear?' He thrust a well-used handgun into the rabbit's paws and turned on his heel. Trailing a peach-scented cloud, Pronto and the posse tiptoed up the drive to StregaSchloss.

In the late afternoon sun, a great stillness hung over the house, as if the stone itself was basking in the warmth. Innocent of the impending threat, StregaSchloss with its total absence of alarms and high-tech security systems, represented a burglar's dream venue. Nobody appeared at windows or doors, no guard dogs lunged at the end of leashes, and the front door stood ajar. There was, however, a long streak of something green and gelatinous smeared across the low bridge over the moat.

The rabbit stroked the muzzle of his handgun and scowled into the sun.

'Not exactly security conscious, are they?' whispered one of the men in black.

'Right,' said Pronto to the knife-wielder. 'You, by the front door as look-out, you round the back, and you and the rabbit in with me through the front door.' Pronto's black-shod foot made contact with the green glop decorating the moat. Immediately the smell of peach air freshener was overcome by something infinitely more unpleasant. The man posted to the back of the house sat down hurriedly on the edge of the moat.

'I feel sick,' he muttered. 'What is that *smell*?'

'Oh here we go again,' moaned the rabbit. 'Wait for it . . .'

'Is that youse?' hissed the knife-wielder, swivelling round from his station by the front door. 'If you've done something in your breeks again, I'm going to install ventilation in yon bunny costume.'

'Cool it,' muttered Pronto, glaring at his besmirched shoe. 'It's not the rabbit, it's this green stuff.'

'I'd hate to meet whatever did that,' said the man

at the front door, picking his teeth with his knife blade.

Gazing nervously around themselves, Pronto and his posse neglected to look upwards. On wobbly wings, Ffup was on the home flight. Whatever had been in last night's smoked hiccup was responsible for the worst case of dragon diarrhoea he'd encountered in 600 years. Ffup was hoping to make it back to his dungeon without another recurrence, but as his wings bore him closer to home, he realized that this was not to be . . .

'Bombs away!' he yelled, swooping low over StregaSchloss. He saw little figures on the ground fleeing from the large green projectile that was speeding their way.

'And a direct hit, if I'm not mistaken,' he observed to himself.

With a tremendous slapping sound, Ffup's digestive overload landed on a human target. There was a scream, a ghastly choking sound and then silence.

Close to the epicentre, the man on the edge of the moat groaned deeply, sank his face into his hands and began to rock backwards and forwards, clutching his machine gun and moaning as he did so. In the reeds at the far side of the moat something stirred. Something that hadn't eaten a nanny for weeks, never mind a gangster . . .

'Come on,' commanded Pronto, breathing shallowly through his mouth. He stepped carefully round the vast green puddle at the front door. 'We've got a job to do. No time for sentimentality. Hey. You,' he pointed to the man by the moat, 'take over at the door.'

'This wasn't in the contract,' muttered the rabbit, his tongue suddenly freed by the demise of the knife-wielder. 'No-one warned *me* about low-flying dragon poo. No-one, come to think of it, so much as mentioned dragons.' Regarding the slimy body of his fallen colleague with horror, he followed Pronto into StregaSchloss. As the front door closed behind them, there came a loud splash as Tock discovered the gastronomic delights of raw gangster with a light garnish of machine gun.

The Hot Toddy Revisited

Low bars of afternoon sunshine slanted through the windows of StregaSchloss, doing little to dispel the atmosphere of gloom in Titus's bedroom. Unaware that their home was being invaded, Titus and Pandora sat in front of the computer screen. Titus felt awful. No matter which keys he pressed or files he opened, he couldn't find a way to locate Damp. Who am I trying to kid, he thought, sending a spider off down a modem into the mother of all webs? There's no *way* Tarantella'll find her. Face facts, pal, you're in trouble. You need bigger, more qualified help than a talking spider with a knowledge of terrestrial webs . . .

Pandora gazed hopelessly into space. Her eyes focused on nothing as she chewed her last fingernail, trying not to start crying again. It's hopeless, she thought, we don't know what we're doing, Tarantella doesn't know where she's going, and Damp is probably lost for ever. At this point, a vast wave of unhappiness swept over her, and she began to cry.

'Come *on*, Pandora,' said Titus, wrapping an arm round his weeping sister. 'We've got to face up to this. We need help.'

Pandora's shoulders heaved.

'I'm going to tell Mum,' Titus decided. 'We can't handle this on our own.'

Pandora's face appeared from behind her hands. Her eyes were pink, her nose ran and her face was awash with tears. Titus doubted if it was humanly possible to look more miserable than his sister did at this moment. 'Mum'll kill us,' she whispered.

'Yup,' agreed Titus, adding illogically, 'but it'll be worth it to get Damp back.'

'I'd do *anything* for that,' sobbed Pandora.

'I *know*,' said Titus, patting her back. 'I'd do anything as well. She may be small and smelly, but she's *ours*, our baby sister.'

'I miss her,' howled Pandora, 'even if she does take up all the bed.'

'Me too,' said Titus, his voice wobbling dangerously near to a sob. 'Don't worry, Mum'll know what to do.'

They stood outside Signora Strega-Borgia's

bedroom, unsure of what to do next.

'You go first,' said Titus. 'You tell her.'

'I'd rather you did,' said Pandora.

'No, you tell her. You look *really* sad, she'll feel sorry for you,' said Titus. 'I look too normal, she'll think I don't care or something.'

'MUM,' sobbed Pandora, opening the door and starting to cry again. 'Mum, something awful's happened . . .'

Signora Strega-Borgia lay across her bed, a huge smile on her face. She hiccuped, rolled onto her stomach, and fell onto the carpet, still smiling. 'Oopsee,' she said. 'Shilly me. Shorry darlingsh, Mummy's a bit shquiffy.' For some reason, she appeared to find this enormously funny, and she rolled around on the carpet, roaring with laughter at her own wit.

Titus was horrified. 'She's *drunk*,' he hissed.

'Legleshh,' agreed Signora Strega-Borgia, over-hearing Titus's comment. 'Drunk ash a shkunk. Wheeeee. Dear Mishish McLachlan and her hot toddy. Hot toddy. Soddy soddy, lots of toddy.' She rolled to a halt at Pandora's feet and gazed upwards at her daughter. 'Wosha matter, darling?' she slurred. 'You look a bit upshet. Bit shad? Down in the dumpsh?'

Pandora sank to her knees, still crying. 'We've lost Damp,' she began. 'On the computer. I borrowed one of your spells, shrank Damp and she ended up in the modem.'

Titus looked at Pandora in admiration. She didn't mention my part in the disappearance of Damp, he thought. Mind you, he added, nor did she mention Multitudina's . . .

'Modem, shmodem,' said Signora Strega-Borgia unhelpfully. 'That'sh your father'sh department. Me, I'm jusht a shimple witshhh, no interesht what-shoever in technoloshy.'

'But Mum – we've lost *Damp*. She's vanished.'

Pandora watched as her mother heaved herself across the carpet and hauled herself inelegantly back into bed. She picked up her pillow, gazed at it in apparent adoration and kissed it tenderly before placing it on the bed beside her. With a little smile she pulled the covers up to her chin. 'Ashk your father,' she said, closing her eyes. 'He'sh good with computersh. And don't worry about Damp,' she added, patting her pillow lovingly. 'She'sh quite shafe here with Mummy, aren't you pet?'

Titus and Pandora stood unbelievingly by their mother's bedside, watching until her heavy breath-ing turned into loud snores. In a state of shock, they tiptoed backwards out of the bedroom. In floods of tears, Pandora fled to the bathroom.

'She was *drunk*,' muttered Titus as he stormed upstairs. 'I've *never* ever seen her do that before. She was disgustingly, dreadfully, horribly, revolt-ingly DRUNK!' Titus burst into tears and sat down abruptly on the stairs. I can't handle this, he thought, first Dad does a bunk, then Damp vanishes and now ... He gripped one of the balustrades as if he wished to throttle it. Fathers aren't supposed to leave their children, baby sisters aren't supposed to shrink and vanish into the ether and mothers are definitely *not* supposed to get drunk. Holding the balustrade for support, Titus stood up. Wearily, as if he carried a huge weight on his shoulders, he wiped his eyes with his sleeve and headed for his bedroom. Closing the door firmly behind him, Titus looked around himself. His bedroom afforded little comfort. No solutions leapt out at him from the overcrowded bookcase. He didn't own any manuals on how to find missing babies. The afternoon sun shining in through the window failed to raise his spirits, and only served as a reminder that Damp had been missing for several hours. His unmade bed seemed to be the sleeping place of some other, younger version of himself. The model aeroplanes dangling from the ceiling on dusty threads were made by some other, younger Titus. With the disappearance of his father and now Damp, Titus felt that his childhood was over. Something has to be done, he resolved. Help has to be found.

He sat down heavily in the chair in front of his computer, and began to type a message to his father.

signor strega-borgia at
dad@mafia.org.ital

dad

we're in trouble. damp is lost, mum is drunk and we need your help. please can you come home immediately? and no more sad kidnap stuff. this is serious.

love

titus

He pressed ENTER, but nothing happened. He pressed it again, but still nothing. No reassuring 'Message Sent' box, just his own letter hanging there on the blue screen.

'Oh GREAT!' yelled Titus. 'Just what I need. Come *on*. Do it for me. Just this once. *Please.*'

Unknown to Titus, inside the modem a minute speck of fly wing dropped by the outgoing Tarantella lay across a vital part of the circuitry. This was causing Titus's message to pause in its journey, shriek to a halt, perform a speedy u-turn and head back to base with the happy news that the information superhighway was now blocked. Also unknown to Titus, this was one of those occasions when a swift thwack to the modem would have solved the problem. However, Titus had been brought up to seek logical solutions, rather than those of brute force. In vain, he opened files, scrolled through Help directories and trawled through computer manuals before laying his head on the keyboard and conceding defeat.

His sister was lost, his mother drunk and his father uncontactable. Concluding that there was nothing more that *he* could do, Titus loaded *Death & Destruction II* and began to plan his assault on Nettlefold.

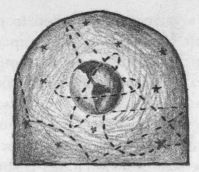

Tarantella Does
the Biz

Routed from StregaSchloss.co.uk to dad@
mafia.org.ital, Damp had one brief glimpse of
her father's face before being whizzed off to
the website for The Really Authentic Italian Food
Company, known to its many clients worldwide as
spag.bol@mamma.

Here was the place where you logged on to order
pasta by the square kilometre. Here was where you
could, should you wish, order up a pizza the size of
the London Underground.

Damp huddled in a corner of a monitor, and
looked out. Launched onto the Internet before
lunchtime, she was now extremely hungry. The
sight of so much food reminded her that she'd
missed a meal. Wishing to share this discovery, she
pressed her face up against the glass of the screen,

and began to grizzle. This failed to produce the desired result. No-one scooped her up and bore her off to the kitchen, bib and bowl. Damp turned up her volume a bit. Nobody noticed. Resorting to desperate measures, Damp flung herself around, thrashing her arms and legs and uttering a brain-curdling shriek. Unfortunately, since she was currently the size of an atom, her best efforts were little louder than a whisper.

Her tiny body connected with an outgoing e-mail, and before she could blink, she found herself once more hurtling along the information super-highway like a human tumbleweed. Damp closed her eyes, opened her mouth, and howled. She whizzed along telephone wires, under the sea, along deep sea communication cables, and occasionally was bounced up into outer space via satellites. Lights flashed past, electricity hummed and computers shrieked like strangulated pea-cocks. Damp was thoroughly dizzy and deafened. Abruptly she came to a near standstill. She swung back and forth, at first in a wide arc, and then slower and slower in decreasing swings till finally she came to a complete halt.

A voice spoke. A friendly, furry, almost familiar voice. 'Damplette!' it said. 'Little Dampy-Pops! She of the nappied *derrière*. Oh, the *trouble* I've had trying to find you. I've been to banks in Bogota, nuclear bunkers in Nevada, supermarkets in Surrey and it was by sheer chance that I fancied some

fettuccine with flies for lunch and found you here
... My mission, should I choose to accept it, is to
return you to your siblings who, even as we dangle
here on the World Wide Web, are sitting weeping,
willing your safe return, wailing and waiting to
welcome you home.'

Damp opened her eyes for a quick peek at the
owner of the voice. Overhead, a gigantic spider
smiled down at her. Damp instantly squeezed both
eyes shut.

'Awww. C'mon, Small,' Tarantella coaxed. 'I
know I've got eight legs and probably more hair
than you've had in your lifetime, but really, I'm on
your side.' She patted Damp's head reassuringly.

Damp flinched, and squeezed her eyes even
tighter shut.

'Oooh Baby,' crooned Tarantella, 'how about a
lullaby?

Poor little Damper
squashed in a Pamper
shrunk to the size of a bug.
Along came a spider
and dangled beside her
and gave her a huge hairy hug.'

Damp burst into tears.

'Oh, I'm sorry. Sorrysorrysorry,' cried Tarantella.
'I didn't mean to frighten you. Don't cry, you'll
short-circuit the Web. C'mon, pet, just think of me
as a black woolly rug, and climb on board ...'

A little howl escaped Damp's lips.

'Oh dear. Desperate measures for desperate times,' muttered Tarantella, beginning to spin.

Damp sat, eyes squinched shut, mouth compressed to a rosebud pucker, trying to ignore the fact that she was being steadily wrapped in spider silk.

'The problem with the younger generation . . .' panted Tarantella as she spun around the baby, '. . . is that you still buy into that Miss Muffet stuff. Haven't you heard of *Charlotte's Web*, or *James and the Giant Peach*?' She stood back to admire her handiwork. 'Purrfect,' she crooned, tucking the silk-swaddled baby under one leg. 'And now . . .'

She stepped backwards, onto the cyberspace equivalent of the fast lane, and was immediately swallowed up in traffic. 'WHEEEEEEEE!'

They crossed continents, traversed oceans and navigated through outer space, and one hour later, at an indecent speed, were bounced into StregaSchloss. Crawling out of the modem and into the CD-ROM, Tarantella paused in the drawer and listened.

She could make out two voices. The one belonging to Titus sounded breathless and scared. The other, unknown, sounded aggressive and very close at hand. It said, 'Buongiorno, Titus. Your Uncle Lucifer sends you this greeting.' A loud bang and a scream convinced the spider that she should stay where she was. Chewing thoughtfully on the speck of fly-wing that she had dropped on her outward journey, Tarantella looked down at her cocooned charge. Damp was oblivious to her surroundings and had fallen asleep during the journey home. The spider was no stranger to motherhood, even if the child appeared to be short of six legs. She patted Damp with a hairy leg, hugged her closer and settled down to wait until it was safe to emerge. Beneath her the circuitry in the computer sprang to life. Without a manual or even a Help directory, Tarantella had fixed Titus's computer problem. She'd simply eaten it.

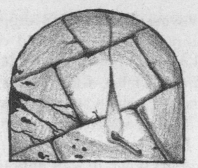

A Gory Bit

No sounds penetrated the walls of the dungeon at StregaSchloss. It was here, amid the restful drip of water on stone, that Latch frequently took his afternoon nap. Stretched out on a pile of straw with the day's paper across his face, he was blissfully unaware that StregaSchloss was under siege.

Nearby, Sab was too involved with his own discomfort to notice anything amiss. His stomach growled and rumbled, trying vainly to digest the previous night's smocked hiccup.

In a far corner, Ffup groaned in his sleep. The dragon had staggered back to his bed in the dungeon, aware that he might be in disgrace after his earlier bombing mission had buried a visitor to StregaSchloss under a mound of green goo.

On Sab's return dungeonwards, he'd found Tock on the Schloss doorstep, polishing off the remains of Ffup's goo and complaining about the lumpy bits. The crocodile smacked his lips and paused to remove machine gun fragments from between his teeth. The shredded remains of a black suit littering the moatside seemed to indicate that Tock had found a pudding to follow his main course.

'Great sauce, this,' he had said, 'but could we sieve out the metal bits next time?'

Just remembering this conversation was enough to make Sab's stomach churn. Rolling his eyes to the ceiling, the gryphon turned himself back into stone. Instantly all activity in his stomach ceased. A slow smile spread across his granite muzzle. His thoughts turned to mountaintops, to pebbles and basalt. Latch's snores and the steady drip of water down the dungeon walls faded from the gryphon's consciousness.

A shadow fell across the bars of the open cage. A shadow cast by a figure dressed in black who was tiptoeing down the dungeon stairs. The figure muttered to himself, cursing as his feet slipped on the mossy stone and he found himself slithering down the remainder of the stairs on his bottom. He arrived at the foot of the stairs, gun clutched in both hands, eyes wide with terror. Staggering to his feet, he blinked in an attempt to see anything in the darkness. 'What kind of a place is this?' he asked himself. The echo answered, this? This? This?

Shifting his gun into one hand, he fumbled forward, using his other hand to feel along the walls. It wasn't long before his trembling fingers found the granite gryphon. As his eyes grew accustomed to the gloom, he could pick out individual features – the flared nostrils, the leonine mane and the eyeballs frozen in their upwards roll.

'The things people keep in their cellars,' he remarked, peering closely at Sab. 'Who in their right mind would want to hang onto an ugly brute like you, pal?'

You pal, you pal, you pal, the echo agreed.

Assuming incorrectly that the dungeon offered no threat whatsoever, the hireling tucked his gun in a holster under his armpit, and leaned back against the gryphon like someone waiting for a passing bus. Furthering this impression of a relaxed commuter, he dangled a cigarette between his lips and rooted in his jacket for a light. He found a single match wedged in the fluff at the bottom of a pocket and searched for a bit of dry stone to strike it on. Reaching upwards, he dragged the match across Sab's eyeball. As the match ignited, the gryphon appeared to undergo a magical transformation, from stone to battered leather. Leather that moved. Leather that reached downwards, and with a brief crunch, neatly removed the hireling's head and spat it across the dungeon. The head landed on the floor beside Latch, its severed nerves and sinews causing it to wink in a horribly life-like fashion.

The remainder crumpled at the knees and pitched forwards onto the dungeon floor. The lit match dropped from a lifeless hand and fizzled out on the floor. Latch awoke from a dream into a nightmare. Lifting the newspaper from his face, he found himself eyeball to eyeball with the head of a headless corpse. A trail of blood led to the corpse which lay leaking gorily under the gryphon. Sab looked up at the dungeon ceiling and tried to whistle.

Latch noted that the gryphon's mouth was suspiciously red and shiny. Bloody, in fact. 'Sab?' Latch's voice came out as a squeak. 'What *have* you done?'

The gryphon stopped whistling and looked down. 'Aaaargh!' he screamed. 'Help! MURDER! Where did *that* come from?' He looked sideways at Latch to see how this was going down. Latch glared at him.

'It's a put-up job!' wailed Sab. 'I've been framed! I'm an innocent bystander! How could you believe that I could do such a thing?'

'Because you've got blood running down your chin,' Latch said grimly.

'Have I?' Sab patted his mouth. 'Oh heck, so I have . . .'

'*Well*?' said Latch. 'What happened?'

'He asked for it,' said the gryphon, folding his arms and trying to look mean.

'What? He actually said, "Please, dear Gryphon, if you're not doing anything too important, could you possibly bite my head off?" ' Latch began to lay pages of his newspaper on the floor, in an attempt to mop up the blood.

'Well . . . not in so many words,' said Sab, avoiding eye contact. 'But I knew he was Up to No Good. Check out the gun in his armpit. Really – you'd have done the same, yourself.'

'Somehow, I very much doubt it,' Latch said under his breath. 'Stay here. Don't move a muscle. I'm going to find Mrs McLachlan.'

As the sound of his footsteps faded away, Sab stood, as instructed, still as a statue. Leathery hide turned back into stone as the gryphon retreated into the state from which he'd been so rudely interrupted. At his feet, the headless gangster resembled a human sacrifice, slain to appease the appetite of an unkind god.

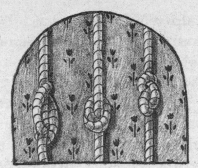

Chilled Attila

Drooling in the kitchen garden, Knot the yeti decided that today was his lucky day. He peered through the kitchen window to check that It was really there. First the discovery of Marie Bain's furry slippers discarded by the range, and now This . . .

In the kitchen, Mrs McLachlan remonstrated with the malodorous bunny as he tied her to a chair with a length of clothes line. 'That knot will never do, dear,' she said. 'Far too easy to undo. Try a double half-hitch-clove-hangman. Much more secure, don't you think?'

'Shut up,' muttered the bunny, adding another granny knot to a chain of knots that dangled like loose knitting from Mrs McLachlan's hands.

'If you don't mind me saying, *dear* . . .'

'I *do*. Shut up, would you?'

'It's for your own good, dear. Something your mother forgot to tell you . . .'

'Shut up, woman, or I'll gag you.'

'As I was trying to say, dear, you mustn't shun soap and water. A bath once a day might not be amiss, either. Oh dear, how can I put this without causing offence? Could you not stand quite so close to me, dear, it's just that you . . . smell rather strange.'

From the other side of the window, Knot nodded in agreement. Deliciously strange, he thought, rancidly yummy, in fact. With a little whimper of anticipation, the yeti burst into the kitchen, spraying a mist of drool around himself. The rabbit turned round just in time to see the yeti lumbering towards him, arms outstretched.

'WHAT the . . .?' he screamed, as Knot grabbed him with both paws, stuffed him head first into his dripping mouth and poked his thrashing feet in afterwards with both thumbs.

'Oh, Knot . . .' said Mrs McLachlan sadly. 'How could you?'

The yeti gulped apologetically, and gazed at Mrs McLachlan with sorrowful eyes.

'After being so ill this morning, dear. You really should give your tummy time to recover . . .'

The yeti gave a small belch and tried to look chastened. Mrs McLachlan wriggled and squirmed in her seat. 'We've got a problem at StregaSchloss,

Knot,' she explained, as she flexed and strained at the knotted washing line. Her feet came undone, closely followed by both hands. 'Unwelcome guests. My horoscope was quite right about that, except it isn't lice, it's a particularly vicious kind of Rat.'

She stood up, the washing line falling to the floor in coils. 'There isn't time to put down poison for this kind of Rat, is there?'

The yeti shook his head in what he hoped was an intelligent fashion. He could have turned cart-wheels for all the notice Mrs McLachlan took of him.

'NO,' she said, opening her large handbag and rummaging in its depths. 'No, Knot, we have to STAMP the vermin out. Eradicate them. Exterminate them. Wipe them off the face of the planet. There's only one thing for it . . .'

Her eyes have gone all funny, Knot thought. Wish I knew what she was on about.

'We need to take them by surprise,' continued Mrs McLachlan. 'Can't very well just barge in through the door, can we? They'd hear us coming.'

Turning her back on Knot to shield her secret from him, Mrs McLachlan withdrew a small perspex box from her handbag. I'm really left with no alternative, she decided, unclipping its lid to reveal the keyboard beneath. This situation is out-with my job description, and regrettably I *have* to use all the powers at my disposal to put it to rights.

Even if those include the use of magic.

With a grim little smile she scanned the kitchen for a suitable candidate for the box's transformative powers. Deciding on the upright freezer, she opened its door and propped her box on top of a bag of frozen chicken legs. The exposed keyboard began to frost over. Mrs McLachlan began to type: F.R.E.E.Z.E.R. Her fingertips left thawed impressions on the frosty keys. Pressing a key named REPLACE, she then typed: S.E.C.R.E.T. P.A.S.S.A.G.E. On a miniature screen on the reverse side of the open lid the prompt appeared: FROM KITCHEN TO WHERE?

Mrs McLachlan didn't hesitate. Her fingers a blur on the keyboard, she typed: T.O. T.I.T.U.S.'.S. B.E.D.R.O.O.M.

'Please, please, let this *not* bring the kitchen wall crashing down around our ears,' Mrs McLachlan begged and holding her breath, she pressed ENTER, snatched her chilly box from the frozen embrace of the chicken legs and slammed the freezer door shut. There was a muffled explosion, the sound of passages opening up in StregaSchloss where no passages existed before. There was a distant grinding noise and then silence, save for the dripping sound of Knot's drool pattering on the kitchen floor. Hearing the sound of approaching footsteps from the direction of the cellar, Mrs McLachlan slipped the box into her pocket and hid in the pantry.

Latch ran into the kitchen, leaving a trail of bloody footprints across the floor. 'Mrs McL . . . Flora,' he hissed in a piercing whisper.

Multitudina bolted out of the pantry, followed by Mrs McLachlan. She stared at the trail of blood behind the butler, took in his startled expression and pale face and instantly understood.

'You have the look of a man who has just found something exceedingly nasty in the dungeon,' she stated.

'Sab beheaded somebody downstairs,' shuddered Latch. 'It . . . he . . . he had a gun.'

'Knot ate the one that was tying me to a chair in the kitchen. He too had a gun.' Mrs McLachlan swallowed. 'We have a problem.'

'Several, I imagine,' Latch agreed.

'There's probably more of them and they're undoubtedly armed,' said Mrs McLachlan, stroking the box in her pocket.

'Where are the children?' Latch's voice rose to a shriek.

'That is what we're going to find out,' muttered Mrs McLachlan, opening the freezer door.

Inside, a narrow staircase wound its way upwards into darkness. Knot stared after them in some confusion. Why keep a staircase in the freezer? he wondered dimly. And, more to the point, where did the chicken legs go? Also in a state of some confusion, Latch bleated, 'Since when was there a secret pass . . .?' Mrs McLachlan cut this short by dragging Latch by the hand into the transformed freezer and pushing him ahead of herself, upstairs.

Knot shuffled forwards, sniffing Latch's trail of bloody footprints more from habit than appetite. From upstairs came the faint stutter of gunfire. The door to the secret passage was shut firmly in his face.

Something Wicked
This Way Comes

Two rolls of soggy toilet paper later, Pandora decided that she'd cried enough to last her entire lifetime. She quietly opened the bathroom door and sought refuge in her bedroom.

Finding her mother drunk and seeing her brother in tears had completely shattered her belief in her family. Nothing could ever be the same again. They had all been so happy . . . once upon a time.

Hadn't they? Her parents had seemed to love each other, or was that just wishful thinking? Pandora needed reassurance desperately, she needed to see proof positive that there had been happiness, that they had been a family. Then, perhaps, then she could find a path back to better times . . . a way to turn the clock back. She hunted along her bookshelves until she found a photograph album that she had shrunk earlier to the size of a thumbnail.

Clumsily leafing through the tiny book, she came across a recent photograph, taken on Damp's first birthday. Peering at the minute picture, she could just about pick out the family group, their pinhead-sized faces gathered round a birthday cake the size of a crumb.

They all looked so small . . . so far away.

They'd been a family then, Pandora thought miserably, observing the microscopic smiles, the air of happiness that permeated the photograph. Three months ago. Only three months and a world can turn itself inside out and upside down. Three months ago Dad was still around, Damp was just an ordinary-sized baby and Mrs McLachlan hadn't moved in . . . And now . . . this postage stamp image was all that remained. Dad had gone, Mum was absent due to being drunk, Damp was lost and Titus . . .

Pandora sighed. Titus, she decided, Titus had lost himself in that damn computer. When he wasn't playing stupid games on it, he was *thinking* about playing stupid games on it. Pandora stood up. She pulled the last Disposawand from her pocket. A vague plan had begun to take shape in her mind. What if, she wondered, a wild grin flitting across her face, what if I *shrink* the computer? Then Titus won't be able to play on it and he'll have to do something about Dad and Mum and . . . Pandora's face fell ... and Damp. Bother. How do we get Tarantella and Damp back if the computer's the size of a matchbox? Bother bother ... Absently sucking the end of her wand, Pandora opened her bedroom door and sleepwalked out into the corridor, her mind full of a plan.

There *must* be a way to do this, she reasoned as she walked slowly towards Titus's room. There *has* to be a way ... shrink the computer, but YES! That's IT! Keep the modem and the CD-ROM the same size. YES YES YES, what a *brain*, Pandora, what a *star*, what a child *prodigy*. Pandora was so captivated by her own brilliance that she was through the door of Titus's bedroom before she realized that he had a visitor. On reflection, she thought, *not* a visitor, an intruder.

Titus's eyes met hers. In his gaze Pandora read fear, pain and utter misery. Without thinking, she raised her left hand and began to draw lazy circles in the air with her wand.

'Right, kid,' Pronto said, waving his gun. 'Over here, don't make a squeak or your brother's a human colander.'

'He means it,' muttered Titus. 'Just do as he says, Pan.'

Pandora advanced on Pronto, her wand poised to cast the spell.

'And put that stick down,' added Pronto. 'It's making me nervous.'

'This old thing?' Pandora said innocently, gazing

at the wand as if she'd just noticed it. 'Here – catch!'

Titus flinched and braced himself. The wand flew through the air towards Pronto who was completly taken aback. Reflexively he thrust out his gun to knock the wand out of the air. The wand and the gun made contact. There was a dazzling flash. Titus and Pandora reeled backwards, their frazzled eyeballs temporarily out of order as after-images of intense light seared their retinas. Blinking frantically, Pandora was first to sense that everything had not gone according to plan. Contrary to what she'd imagined when she cast her spell, Pronto was *not* holding a miniaturized firearm, capable only of immobilizing ladybirds and bruising craneflies.

Pronto gazed at his outstretched arm, a nasty grin stretched across his face. He no longer held a small machine gun. Instead, Pronto was stroking the oily barrel of the deadliest automatic weapon known to man. So sophisticated, it didn't have a trigger, it picked up signals from the user's brain. So advanced, it didn't have a telescopic sight, it had an infra-red flesh-detector to locate and lock on to its target. Such a deadly weapon that its inventor had turned it on himself in a fit of remorse for having created such a lethal artefact. Its name was Wormwood and it lay, hissing quietly in Pronto's arms, its blind snout jerking from side to side as it located first Pandora and then Titus.

'Oh well DONE,' Titus said bitterly, 'What a

GENIUS. What a STAR you are, sister dear.'

Pandora rubbed her eyes and glared at her brother. 'It's that wand,' she wailed, 'I did everything right, but the *wand* didn't work.'

'This old thing?' Pronto purred, picking up the fallen wand and examining it. *'Contrawand,'* he read, *'reverses spells, undoes charms and nixes hexes.* Hang on there's something else written on it in very small letters. *The manufacturers recommend six uses only before safe disposal as hazardous magical waste.'*

Pandora's shoulders slumped.

'Well . . . ?' demanded Titus.

'Actually,' admitted Pandora, 'the wand worked perfectly.'

'I'll second *that,'* gloated Pronto, patting Wormwood. From the gun came a ghastly sound like forks being dragged aross a plate.

The children shuddered.

'Right,' Pronto continued, addressing Titus, 'where were we before we were so charmingly interrupted? Ah yes, UP AGAINST THE WALL AND SAY YOUR GOODBYES.'

A Pound of Flesh

D on Lucifer di S'Embowelli gazed at his reflection in the mirror. Dressed in a lilac hospital gown with a disposable paper hat covering his skull, he was aware that he did not look at his best. This impression was supported by the fact that his vast nose was covered in blue lines and words like 'nip', 'tuck', 'slash' and 'tear along the dotted line'. These scrawled instructions together with the grid of blue lines made the Don's nose resemble a street map drawn in haste on the back of a napkin. Very undignified, the Don thought, but it will all be worth it. Today I go under the knife of Italy's top plastic surgeon, Professore Flense-Filleto. Not only will he sculpt me the perfect nose but he and his team of doctors and nurses will provide me with a perfect alibi. The

Don permitted himself the tiniest of smiles, imagining that evening's newspaper reports:

DON KNIFED
WHILE BROTHER CRISPED

Don Lucifer di s'Embowelli was undergoing surgery in an exclusive Milanese hospital while a mysterious fire broke out at his secluded Palazzo. Firemen called to the scene arrived too late to rescue the Don's beloved brother Luciano from the inferno which razed the Palazzo to the ground.

Police sources reveal that the Don is not under suspicion.

Don Lucifer bared his teeth in a feral grin. Perfect. With all witnesses able to swear that on the day of the 'accident', the main suspect had booked himself into their hospital for a major rhinoplasty, there was little that the police could do to pin the 'mysterious fire' on him. Perfect. A masterplan, in fact.

There was a discreet knock at the door. The Don leapt across the room and arranged himself on the bed. Professore Flense-Filleto swung into the room, followed by a posse of young doctors and nurses.

'We're ready for you now, Signor di S'Embowelli,'

said the Professore. 'All the knives are razor sharp and I've been practising my sewing on an old bit of chamois leather, har dee har, fnaar fnaar.'

Obediently, the posse broke out in forced laughter. The Don paled. Propelled by three nurses, his bed began to move slowly across the room.

Opening the door, the Professore oozed confidence. 'Not nervous, are we? Mustn't mind my little jokes. We've got a lovely little elephant's trunk just waiting for you in theatre, haven't we, nurse? Haar haar, fnaar.'

Wearily, the posse sniggered on cue. The Don sat bolt upright in bed. Pushing him back into a horizontal position, the Professore continued, 'Nothing can possibly go wrong, Signor. We have technology at our fingertips. We'll hook you up to our machines, everything computer-controlled and linked to several hospitals across the world, and *that* way we have the skills of many of the finest surgeons at our disposal. You could say that you are at the cutting edge of science, hurr hurr hurr.'

The nurses gave the Don's bed a particularly vicious push, and he found himself barrelling through the doors to the theatre.

'Just a little jab and you'll soon drift away,' one of the nurses said, bending over the bed and slipping a needle into the Don's arm. She straightened up and began sorting scalpels and forceps. 'Count backwards from ten for me, Signor di S'Embowelli . . . ?'

Obediently, the Don began, 'Ten, nine, eight, seven lawyers, six . . . six policemen, five alive, alive oh, four no more, four sharksss . . . Ragu . . . Lucianoooo . . .'

His eyeballs slid backwards in his head. The Don's last awareness was of straps being placed round his head and arms, and the disembodied voice of the Professore saying, 'Signor, is that a fine pair of sunglasses you're wearing or are those your nostrils? Huurr hurr dee fnaar.'

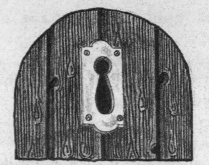

You're Toast

Signor Strega-Borgia clapped a hand to his forehead. This computer infestation was beyond him. He had spent the better part of a working day frantically dismantling computer mainframes, and still the rats eluded him. No sooner would he undo the maintenance panels on one monitor than the rats would disappear from within it with a squeak. Within seconds, they would re-appear on a nearby screen with their pink noses pressed up against the glass in a demented form of peek-a-boo.

To add to his discomfort, the temperature in the computer room was climbing rapidly. Signor Strega-Borgia loosened his tie, removed his jacket and rolled up his shirt sleeves. After a moment, he removed his shoes and socks. The marble floor felt warm underfoot.

'Strange . . .' he muttered, padding across the room to a working terminal. He keyed in stregaschloss.co.uk and stopped. In front of him the cursor blinked, on, off, on, off. If only it was all so simple, he thought, on, off, yes, no. Despite their apparent complexity, computers work on a binary system of choices. On or off were the only options. No in-between choices. No shades of grey. Just two choices. And what if you make the wrong choice, he thought, like that awful day when I stormed out of StregaSchloss, fuelled by a moment's rage . . .

The empty screen waited. Taking a deep draught from a bottle of warm Coke, Signor Strega-Borgia began feverishly to type an e-mail to his son. After a few paragraphs, he found that the sweat trickling down his forehead was stinging his eyes. His shirt stuck to his back and his fingers slithered around on sweaty keys. 'Need some air in here,' he muttered, heading for the door.

PUSH, it read. Signor Strega-Borgia pushed. Nothing happened. Signor Strega-Borgia pushed again. The door remained firmly shut. Signor Strega-Borgia hurled his weight against the door. Still, nothing. Taking several paces backwards, he ran at the door and launched a flying kick at it.

He slowly picked himself up off the floor, checked that no major limbs were broken, and crawled to the door. Pressing his eye up to the keyhole, Signor Strega-Borgia singed his eyelashes on the metal. Disbelieving the evidence of his eyelashes, he felt the keyhole with his hand. 'OUCH!' he yelled. The metal was red hot.

It was at this point that Luciano Strega-Borgia realized that he would never see his family again.

Stripped down to his boxer shorts, Signor Strega-Borgia sat panting at a computer terminal. The temperature in the computer room rose by the minute. Half an hour before, it had been perfect for cooking meringues, now it was the ideal temperature to roast turkey. Large turkeys.

Two tears tracked down his cheeks, evaporating as they slid chinwards. Signor Strega-Borgia was typing what he knew to be his last letter. He paused to wipe his sweat-slippy hands on his discarded shirt. Blinking through his tears, he looked at his words on the screen in front of him: dearest titus, beloved pandora, adored damp and my beautiful wife.

Recalling their faces, he tried not to imagine them held at gunpoint, pale and terrified, his beloved family at the mercy of Pronto. It will be all right, he reassured himself, Lucifer has what he wants and he will call off his hired thugs. Hoping against hope that this was indeed the case, he returned to his e-mail and typed: i shall shortly be leaving you for ever, but before i go, i want to say these few words . . .

titus – my son, my first-born. i loved you

from the moment i heard your newborn wail. as i watched you grow from an infant into a fine young man, my love grew daily. be brave, my son, be true

Signor Strega-Borgia paused to blow his nose loudly into his shirt. Stifling a sob, he continued: and there's a keyboard shortcut for death and destruction ii that neutralizes the force field round nettlefold. it's control, shift, alt while your left hand holds down option, shift, caps lock. good hunting!

pandora – my darling girl, my eldest daughter. born with the august moon flooding your eyes, you have brought perpetual summer into my life. your regal dignity surrounded you since you were a tiny baby, my princess. be brave, my love and remember – at least this way, i won't embarrass you when you grow up.

one last thing – no pierced ears, noses or whatever until you're at least 21, and *that's* final.

and

damp – my little baby, my sweetest flower. by the time you are old enough to read this yourself, you won't remember me at all.

He paused again, struck by the thought that for his youngest child he would be nothing. Not even a vague memory. A blank dada. The thought was not a happy one. The soles of his feet began to feel uncomfortably hot, so perched on a melting stool, he carried on.

you'll have to ask your mama about me. ask her about raspberries blown on your tummy, about how we laughed together, about how much i loved you.

may your life be full of flowers, love and laughter. and know this – that your daddy loved you to bits.

He stopped for a short weep. The winking cursor blinked on and off, waiting mindlessly for more words. 'It's so *sad*,' howled Signor Strega-Borgia. 'I won't see any of them grow up. I'll be a blackened crisp while they slowly forget me . . .'

He picked up his shirt, noticing that despite having used it as a giant handkerchief, it was dry . . . and very hot. Blowing his nose yet again, he came to the final part of his farewell letter.

my love, my life, my dearest only wife . . .

He typed frantically for as long as he could, stopping occasionally to pour warm Coke over his head in a hopeless attempt to cool himself down. Finally, he reached the ed of the letter. Sniffing, he typed in the address: my best-loved family@stregaschlosss. co.uk and blowing a kiss to the screen, he pressed ENT and ER. To his relief, up on the screen came the reassuring words: MESSAGE SENT.

Emptying the last drops of Coke over his head, Signor Strega-Borgia sat and waited for death.

The Music of
the Pipes

Pronto's arms ached with the weight of the
gun, Wormwood. 'Come *on*,' he groaned.
'How long does it take to say goodbye?'

'A long time if you're a Strega-Borgia,' muttered
Pandora.

'You see, we have to say it in Urdu, Serbo-
Croatian, Mandarin . . .' explained Titus.

'Not to mention Xhosa, Pig Latin, Ancient Greek
and Yibble,' added Pandora.

'Two minutes more,' warned Pronto, drumming
his fingers on Wormwood's barrel. 'Don't think I
don't know when I'm having the Michelangelo
taken.'

'Ot-whay ow-nay?' whispered Titus.

'On't-day o-knay,' said his sister, nibbling the
skin round her gnawed fingernails. 'E're-way

oomed-day.' She was trying not to look at Wormwood. In her terror, her eyes scanned round Titus's room, finally alighting on a gloomy oil painting that had hung in the bedroom for as long as she could remember. It was a particularly hideous depiction of a fox, cornered by men in red jackets and fat, drooling hounds. The fox, as could be expected, was looking rather nervous, the hounds somewhat hungry and the red-jacketed men faintly nauseous. The whole had been painted in sombre earth colours of mud, sludge and silage and titled *The unspeakable in pursuit of the inedible*.

It hung on the wall, just behind Pronto, massive and ugly . . . and ever so slightly askew. In fact, not askew, Pandora realized. It looked just like a vast door, slightly ajar . . .

At the top of the secret stairway, Latch and Mrs McLachlan halted. Trying not to sneeze in the dusty air, they whispered to each other in the darkness.

'We'll surprise him,' hissed Latch. 'I'll burst in, tackle him, hurl him to the ground, get his arms up behind his back, kick his gun to one side, frogmarch him downstairs and phone the police . . .'

'Er, no, dear, I *don't* think so,' whispered Mrs McLachlan, discreetly removing her little perspex box from her pocket and flipping it open. 'Too risky – we can't have stray bullets flying around.'

Attempting to shield the box from Latch's enquiring gaze, she switched it on and peered within. It lit up with a silvery glow, illuminating her face and causing Latch to wonder why, at a time like this, his companion had decided to turn girly and powder her nose.

'Have you a better suggestion?' he muttered through clenched teeth. 'For heaven's sake woman, there isn't time to gaze in your mirror, come *on*!' And without waiting for a reply, he burst through the secret door into Titus's bedroom.

Later, Pandora would recall that everything moved very quickly from the moment that she'd noticed the off-kilter painting. One minute she was wondering why it appeared to hang from the wall on hinges, and next thing Latch was flying through it like a . . . well, really, like a *hero*, she admitted, as Latch landed on top of that vile gangster with the horrible gun.

'BANZAIIIiii!' yelled Latch, launching himself at Pronto. 'GERRRRONIMO!' he added for effect, as he knocked Wormwood out of Pronto's grasp.

Pronto was scrabbling across the floor in pursuit of Wormwood, followed by Latch who was intent on fastening his hands around the thug's throat when Mrs McLachlan stepped through the hole in the wall with a dazzling object held in her outstretched hands. A beam of light streamed from it, bathing Pronto in a silver glow.

The gangster flailed and screamed, and Latch, sensing victory, fastened his hands around Pronto's neck.

'Oh for goodness sake!' wailed Mrs McLachlan

as she saw what a ghastly mistake she had made. 'What a *stupid* idiot. What a *moron*. What a cretinous act of cybermagic. What a dumb thing to do.'

'WHAT?' roared Latch, his hands tight round Pronto's throat. 'What have I done *now*, woman?' From beneath him came a ghastly sound like a strangulated wheeze.

'Not you, dear, *me*. I missed. My aim was off.' Mrs McLachlan tutted, closing her perspex box with a snap and instantly dropping it into her pocket. She crossed the room to where Wormwood lay twitching and spinning on the floor. 'This,' she explained, picking up the gun with some difficulty, '*this* was my intended target.'

The gun hissed in her arms, twitching this way and that, seeking skin. 'Revolting thing,' said Mrs McLachlan, reaching under the trigger for the on/off switch. Immediately Wormwood slumped over her arm, floppy as a disk and pliable as a slinky.

Latch gazed at her in some confusion. If the gun hadn't become her target, what had? A snort from Titus caused him to turn back to his wheezing victim.

'Oh, Latch,' gasped Pandora, 'If you could only see your face!' Bewildered, Latch slowly released his grip on the fallen Pronto.

A strangely familiar droning groan came from beneath the butler's kilt. Titus and Pandora made eye contact and burst into hysterical giggles. In a forlorn attempt at maintaining some shred of dignity, Latch rose to his feet, dusted down his kilt and cleared his throat. 'Would someone be kind enough to explain to me why I find myself locked in mortal combat with that . . . that *thing*?' he spluttered, pointing at what lay on the floor at his feet.

Pronto had undergone a magical transformation. Where seconds before he had stood, exuding bristling Mafia menace, now he lay metamorphosed into a giant set of bagpipes, droning like a stale tartan fart.

Titus prodded the ex-thug with his toe. Pronto obliged with a desolate wheeze.

Trying her hardest to keep a serious expression pinned to her face, Mrs McLachlan wrapped an arm round Latch's shoulder, and began to explain what had really happened. 'You see, you were just a wee bitty impetuous, dear. If you'd waited for me, I could have turned that nasty gun into . . .' Seeing the look on Latch's face, Mrs McLachlan hastily changed tack. 'Now, dear, if you hadn't been so brave and rushed in to tackle that brute single-handed . . .' she crooned.

A tiny smile began to hover round Latch's mouth.

'. . . and with no thought for your own personal safety . . .' Mrs McLachlan sighed admiringly.

Bored with all this Latch-flattery, Titus drifted back to his computer screen and discovered that it was now working again. To his delight there was a message informing him that he had mail. Titus downloaded it and began to read while Pandora experimented with the musical possibilities of a metamorphosed thug.

'. . . and the way you dropped him with just one blow – I'm just lost in admiration . . .' murmured Mrs McLachlan in the background.

Pandora leaned over her brother's shoulder to read whatever it was that he was so engrossed in.

'. . . such strong hands you have, and you cut a fine figure in a kilt . . .' somehow Mrs McLachlan was keeping a straight face as she laid the flattery on with a trowel.

'OH NO!' wailed Titus. 'DAD! NO! Help, we've got to do SOMETHING!'

'Somebody get Mum,' yelled Pandora. 'Something awful's about to happen. LATCH! GET MUM! NOW!'

Inside Titus's modem, Tarantella sighed. There they go again, she thought. One drama after another. And so much noise and fuss. She looked down at the sleeping Damp. The baby was oblivious to her siblings' recent near-extinction, her father's imminent crispdom and her mother's inebriation. She slept, slung in the cradle of Tarantella's eight legs, cocooned in spider silk, her mouth slightly open and her cheeks flushed pink from the warmth of the modem's internal workings.

The Revenge of the Hot Toddy

Signora Strega-Borgia proved difficult to wake. 'S'amatter?' she protested as Latch hauled her out of bed and Mrs McLachlan dragged her under a cold shower. 'Wossarush? S'apanic? Aargh! STOP! It's *freezing*! Wossgoinon? Aah! No! STOP THIS!'

Mrs McLachlan, satisfied that her employer was now fully awake, turned off the shower. Signora Strega-Borgia lurched out of the bathroom leaving a trail of wet footprints behind her. The nanny followed, holding out a bath towel by way of a peace offering.

'This had better be good, Mrs McLachlan,' Signora Strega-Borgia said, ignoring the towel and pulling a dressing-gown round herself. 'There had better be a *very* good reason for knocking me out with your fiendish hot toddy, *then* trying to drown me in that . . .'

Mrs McLachlan interrupted, 'Madam, hurry, it's the Master and the wee baby . . .' Her voice broke.

'What is it? Where's Damp? Luciano? Flora, *tell* me. Are they hurt? Injured?' Signora Strega-Borgia's eyes filled. 'Oh *no*. Not dead, *no*! Tell me not. TELL ME THEY'RE NOT DEAD, Flora. FLORA!'

'No, Madam, but . . .'

'Where *are* they?' screamed Signora Strega-Borgia, grabbing Mrs McLachlan's shoulders and shaking her. 'Where ARE they?'

'Oh, Madam,' Mrs McLachlan sobbed, 'they're in the computer.'

'I don't *believe* it!' yelled Signora Strega-Borgia, abruptly releasing Mrs McLachlan's shoulders and pacing round her bedroom, addressing the furniture. 'She drags me out of my sick-bed, half-drowns me in water cold enough to give a polar bear hypothermia, leads me to believe that my baby daughter and missing husband are in mortal danger, and for what? FOR WHAT?' She paused in front of her reflection in the dressing table mirror. 'FOR WHAT?' she bawled.

The mirror rippled and spoke:
>   'Thou art the fairest,
>   as everyone knows,
>   but thou hast iced water
>   dripping off thy nose . . .'

'Shut UP!' yelled Signora Strega-Borgia, continuing through clenched teeth. 'For what, I ask you? Woken, drowned *and* frozen in order to learn that baby and spouse are on the computer. How earth-shattering. How desperately important. How . . .'

'Madam,' interrupted Mrs McLachlan.

'Yes, MRS McLachlan?' said Signora Strega-Borgia in a voice that dripped vitriol. 'What now? Perhaps you need to tell me that . . . let me see . . . it's Saturday? The earth is still turning? Night will follow day?'

Showing remarkable patience in the face of Signora Strega-Borgia's tide of sarcasm, Mrs McLachlan continued, speaking slowly and clearly as if to a small child. 'I said *IN*, Madam, not *on. IN*, as in, "Your husband and daughter are *in* the computer."'

'*What?*' wailed Signora Strega-Borgia. 'No, don't answer. Show me. Please. I don't care *how* they got in there, just take me to them.'

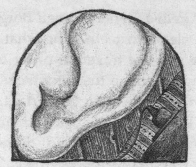

A Muffin-scented Gale

'**T**itus, can you send an e-mail to Dad?'

'Fat lot of good that would do,' said Titus, his eyes glued to his father's last message on the screen. 'E-mail's not going to save him now.'

'Titus! Yes or no? Can we e-mail him?'

'Yes,' sniffed Titus. 'We can. Now. Since the computer seems to be working again. Why? What's the point? What are you doing, Pandora?'

Pandora looked up from where she'd been hunting under her brother's bed. 'Got it.'

'Got what?'

'The wand, Titus. I've got an idea. I'll shrink myself like Damp, and you blow me into the modem, e-mail me to Dad, I'll shrink *him* and . . .'

'Oh BRILLIANT!' yelled Titus. 'Oh Pan, what a

GREAT PLAN! What a STAR! You're a GENIUS!'

'Yes, I have to agree,' said Pandora, circling the wand round and round her body.

'WAIT!' screamed Titus, grabbing her wrist. 'Stand on the modem, or on the table. If you shrink on the floor, I'll never find you.'

'Oops. Good thinking, Titus.' Pandora clambered onto the table and began again. She spun with the wand, slowly at first, and then faster and faster until, with a final thrust, she pointed the wand directly at her heart. 'Oh hell . . .' she wailed.

With a crash, the table beneath her gave way.

'Oh NO,' groaned Titus. 'You forgot, didn't you, dumbo?'

'Contrawand,' moaned Pandora, her gigantic mouth pressed against the plaster cornice of Titus's bedroom ceiling. 'Hang on a tick . . .'

Pandora filled the room.

Her massive feet pressed hard against the bedroom door, her mountainous bottom swamped Titus's bed, and with one colossal fist she plucked her brother off his seat and brought him within range.

'Who're you calling "dumbo"?' she said.

Titus, gazing into an eyeball the size of a watermelon, swallowed painfully. 'N . . . N . . . not you, sister dear.'

'I thought not,' Pandora sighed. 'Listen squirt, much as I'd love to play around with you, we don't have the time, so if you'll be good enough to pass me my wand from under that table . . .'

She gently placed her brother back on the floor and he passed her the wand. In her wardrobe-sized hand, it looked like a matchstick as she made dainty circles round her stomach.

'Careful,' warned Titus. 'Any bigger and you'll go through the roof.'

With a patter of falling plaster, Pandora resumed her normal size.

'*Right*,' she said, spitting out bits of ceiling. 'Let's put the modem on this footstool, and I'll climb up here and . . .'

Round and round she spun the wand, and with a grin for Titus . . . vanished.

'Pan? PANDORA? Oh NO! Now what?' He bent over the footstool, trying hard not to breathe. 'Pandora – yell if you're still here.' He leaned closer to where he hoped his shrunken sister might be, his ear close to the modem.

A tiny voice said, 'Yeuchhh. Don't you ever wash in there? You're so GROSS, Titus.'

'Get ready, Pandora. Curl up in a ball, and that way you might not break too many limbs . . . five, four.' Titus leant carefully over the footstool and stood, fingers poised over the keyboard. He took a deep breath.

'I'm scared, Titus.'

'Three, two, don't be a wuss, Pan, one . . . PUFF! We have lift-off . . .'

There was no applause, no spectacular blast of

smoke. There was just a profound absence of Pandora.

There was a huge muffin-scented gale, sweeping her up, tumbling her over and over. There were spinning colours, a kaleidoscopic whirlpool and then . . . black. There was pain all over as she crashed and bumped into unknown things in the modem. But mainly there was fear. Something breathed in there. More than one thing, in fact.

Pandora had never felt so afraid in her life. What if . . . ? No, don't. Titus called me a wuss. Titus doesn't know the half of it. Give me a couple of lengths with Tock any day. Pull yourself together, girl, somewhere out there are your father, your baby sister and your favourite spi . . .

'TaranTELLA!' shrieked Pandora.

'ShhhHH! *Quiet*,' hissed the spider, clamping a hairy leg over Pandora's mouth. 'You'll wake the baby, and *believe* me, you don't want to do that.' Tarantella shuddered and released Pandora. 'Who ever would have thought that such a hairless little wrinkly could make such a din.'

'Oh, Tarantella, well DONE. You *found* her.' Pandora reached out to stroke Damp's face and stumbled. In front of her a black void opened up.

'Whoa. Careful,' warned Tarantella, snatching Pandora back to safety.

'Fall into that and you could end up *anywhere*,'

she said, opening her eyes wide for emphasis. '*Anywhere.*'

Above their heads, blue flashes of energy crackled. Each flash illuminated the industrial landscape that surrounded them. Giant lentils on spindly legs alternated with vast stripy cylinders poised on metal scaffolds. Perspex skyscrapers perched on a landscape cross-hatched with gleaming metal runways. It was bleak, it was ugly and it was utterly devoid of life.

'Where is this?' whispered Pandora.

'This is the printed circuitboard,' intoned Tarantella, dropping her voice to a whisper and adding, 'that black tunnel into which you so nearly fell, that . . . that is the void, the portal.'

Pandora peered at the spider in the gloom. Tarantella's eyes glowed.

'That's the way in, d'you mean?'

'Dear child, think of it as a slip road, leading onto a great motorway . . . or perhaps a trickling brook that turns into a great river and eventually rushes into the sea . . . or perhaps . . .'

'Tarantella,' interrupted Pandora. 'How do I hitch a lift on an outgoing e-mail?'

'You simply stand in front of one, just like you'd stand in front of a speeding articulated lorry. *Just* like, believe me. Hits you like a ten-ton truck, whizzes you off into the Web, and seconds later, SPLAT, you've arrived.' Seeing Pandora's horrified expression, Tarantella expanded further. 'I imagine it's similar to what flies feel when they're spread across a windscreen. One minute buzz buzz . . . and the next thing that goes through their minds is their bottom.'

Pandora groaned. Her Rescue Dad Plan appeared to have a serious drawback. But, she thought, hang on a minute . . . 'How come you're not dead? And Damp? You're not both windscreen smears, are you?'

Tarantella arranged herself for a cozy chat. 'What you've failed to grasp, o leggily-challenged one, is that this is *virtual* travel. Not real travel. *Not* the same thing at all.'

Oh heck, thought Pandora. Do Not Pass Go until the spider has delivered an interminable lecture . . .

'Look, hairless one, when you send an e-mail, you're not sending a bit of paper with a letter written on it, are you?'

'No . . . but,' said Pandora, propping her chin on her knees and trying to look interested.

'Nor does your e-mail travel only on cables and wires, does it?'

'Nhuh?' said Pandora, beginning to lose the plot.

'Sometimes it's bounced through space via satellite, or zapped out by microwave . . .'

'Duh,' agreed Pandora. It was warm in the modem. Warm and cozy. She leant back into Tarantella's furry body and watched Damp's eyes roll behind her eyelids.

'. . . so you see it's utterly painless,' droned the

spider. 'If you don't believe me, I'll show you.'

In the vast spaces beyond the confines of the modem, Titus brought his fingers thudding down on the keyboard. Spotting an opportunity to demonstrate the wonders of Web-travel, Tarantella acted swiftly. 'Look, here comes one now. Hang on tight . . .'

Holding Pandora and Damp snug against her abdomen, Tarantella leapt in front of Titus's outgoing message to dad@mafia.org.ital.

Endgame

Death was horribly slow in coming, thought Signor Strega-Borgia. The air in the computer room stank of melting plastic, as one by one the banks of computers surrounding him overheated, sent out onscreen warnings of system errors and, with small puffs of black smoke, went down.

This must be what lobsters feel like as they boil alive, he thought. Droplets of sweat dripped off his nose and hissed as they landed on the floor. The air burned his throat with each breath he took. Forget lobsters, he thought, more like barbecued chicken. To distract himself from his imminent extinction, Signor Strega-Borgia loaded *Revenge IV* into the last working computer. He huddled on a chair, curled in a ball, waiting for the game to run.

On-screen came a menu: CHOOSE YOUR WEAPON it read.

NUCLEAR WARHEAD

NAIL-STUDDED CLUB

RUSTY DAGGER

VIAL OF VITRIOL

BOX OF DYNAMITE

'Oh very good,' groaned Signor Strega-Borgia, as the last choice scrolled past him: FLAMETHROWER.

He armed himself and clicked onto the main menu:

BATTLEGROUND

CHOOSE FROM THE FOLLOWING:

SUPERMARKET ON A SATURDAY AFTERNOON

LONDON TAXI RANK AT 11.20 P.M. ON A RAINY FRIDAY NIGHT

THE OVAL ROOM, WASHINGTON D.C.

PHNING PTUI JUNGLE, SOMEWHERE IN THE SUBTROPICS

Signor Strega-Borgia sighed. For some reason this game was failing to hold his attention. He gazed blankly at the screen where little figures armed with nail-studded clubs were invading the fish counter in a busy supermarket. A message box appeared: YOU HAVE MAIL.

Signor Strega-Borgia stared at the message. He wondered who on earth it was from as his fingers slid across the keyboard. He found the Open Mail command and pressed ENT and ER. Maybe he could ask for help. Maybe it was the local Fire

Brigade e-mailing the Palazzo, to enquire why it was belching smoke and flames all over the rural Italian countryside. Maybe it was one of his evil half-brother's associates, checking that he'd melted. He glared at the screen, willing it to hurry up and download this unknown message. Another box appeared on-screen:

MESSAGE DELIVERED
REPLY?

'*What* message?' wailed Signor Strega-Borgia. 'There's nothing there. It's empty. It's BLANK!'

Over the crackle and hiss of the encroaching inferno came a tiny squeaking sound. '*Not* the rats,' moaned Signor Strega-Borgia. 'Burned to a crisp in the company of several roasted rodents is *not* a nice way to go.'

The etheric journey to the Palazzo was swift and brutal. Pandora's eyelids were dragged back into her skull and her eyes streamed. It was *exactly* like being a bug stuck to the windscreen of a speeding articulated lorry. Space whooshed past her, deafening, blinding and utterly terrifying. In the midst of the technological maelstrom, she caught a brief flash of something strangely familiar ... Several somethings, in fact.

Heading on a collision course towards Tarantella, Damp and Pandora were the missing rat babies, their yellow teeth bared in the airflow, their tails streaming out behind them. Just as it seemed inevitable that the two parties of e-travellers should collide, the ratlets veered off to the left and vanished. Almost immediately, with an excruciatingly jarring impact, Pandora, Damp and Tarantella arrived at the portal. The spider nimbly dragged her cargo onto a ledge, from where they could look down in safety onto the endless rush of traffic below.

'*There*,' said Tarantella, 'now you know. Just give me a minute to powder my nose and I'll take you back home.'

'Where are we now?' groaned Pandora, checking herself for breakages.

'Does it matter?' said the spider, producing a tiny mirror from a hidden pouch, and peering at her reflection. 'Let's return this baby to where she belongs *before* she wakes up . . .'

'I can't go back yet,' whispered Pandora. 'I have to find Dad.'

'You've lost your father?' muttered Tarantella through a mouthful of lipstick. She puckered up at her reflection with a kissing sound and continued, 'How very careless of you . . . I ate mine.'

Pandora shuddered. 'Where's the way out?' she said.

'Up thataway,' said the spider, indicating a steep tunnel leading away from their ledge.

Pandora stood up and hugged Tarantella.

'Awwwk. My lipstick . . .' moaned the spider. 'What was *that* for?'

'Look after Damp till I return,' said Pandora, 'and if I'm not back in twenty minutes, go home without me.'

'Now hang *on* a minute,' the spider said, her eyes growing saucer-like with alarm. 'You're *not* leaving me with this baby. No *way*. It might leak, it might smell, it might . . . WAKE UP AGAIN. No, no, NO. Wherever you go, I'll be right behind you.'

'I hoped you'd say that,' Pandora smirked. 'Come on then, this way.'

Together they scrabbled up the tunnel towards the light. Tarantella pushed Pandora onwards when the tunnel climbed steeply. Damp rocked from side to side, swaying under the spider's abdomen, rocked in a hairy cradle.

'It's getting hotter,' Pandora said, stating the obvious. The sides of the tunnel were no longer hard and cool. Each step they took sank into warm rubbery stickiness. 'It's like wading through treacle,' she moaned.

'Nearly there,' gasped Tarantella.

At last they arrived in a challenged version of the modem at StregaSchloss. Puddles of plastic oozed from the ceiling, melting giant lentils swayed on red hot legs, giant wires glowed white beneath their feet, and they ran in the direction of the light.

* * *

The squeaking grew louder. Signor Strega-Borgia slumped in front of the screen. To the smell of burning plastic would soon be added the odour of crispy rat. It was unbearable. He buried his face in his hands and wept.

Through his tears he saw something tiny move by the modem. Something small, growing bigger ... and bigger and bigger with each blink of his unbelieving eyes. It yelled. It wailed. It groaned.

'DAD!'

'Bwaaaaaaa ...'

'Oh Lord, here we go again, pat pat, rock rock, soothe pat.'

'PanDORA!' screamed Signor Strega-Borgia, automatically brushing the spider off his desk. 'DAMP!'

'Don't mind me,' muttered Tarantella, 'I'm just the substitute nanny. What's the odd broken leg when one has so many ... OUCH! This floor's *roasting*!'

She sprang onto an unmelted chair and glared at the tender reunion taking place in front of her.

'Oh, DAD.'

'Oh, DARLINGS, oh my little *girls*, Pandora, Damp.'

Not so little, thought Pandora with relief. In fact, normal size, thank heavens.

'Great,' said the spider, 'now that we've established who we all are, can we leave? Please?

I, for one, am not equipped for such a heat wave.'

'We have to get *out* of here,' said Pandora, looking doubtfully at her wand.

Tarantella began a slow handclap.

Six uses only, it had said. In a panic, she counted: One-Pronto/Wormwood, Two-herself (huge), three-herself (normal), four-herself (microscopic), five-Damp, Tarantella and herself (normal). She needed to use it two more times. Once to shrink them all for the journey home, and one last time to return them to life-size once they arrived safely at StregaSchloss. That made seven. She bit her lip and decided.

'We have to risk it. Hold Damp, grab onto me and . . .'

Tarantella jumped into Pandora's arms. Signor Strega-Borgia grabbed Damp. The door to the computer room burst into flames.

'QUICK!' screamed Pandora. 'Hold on TIGHT!'

She spun the wand, round and round, faster and faster. Damp opened her mouth wide and screamed. Blinding smoke poured into the room. Tarantella choked and spluttered, and in her panic, wrapped all eight of her legs tightly round Pandora's nose.

Faster and faster. In the computer room, the lights flickered and went out.

'RUN!' yelled Pandora.

Coughing and sobbing, they waded through the

melting modem, fell down the tunnel and out onto the ledge. With a final howl from the terrified Damp, they threw themselves off the ledge, and fell screaming, down into the stream of traffic.

A Bit of a Mix-up

Signora Strega-Borgia sat chewing her fingernails, peering at the screen on Titus's computer. For the tenth time she asked, 'How long *now*? D'you think they'll be all right? Can't you send me too?'

Titus groaned.

'I can't stand this. Waiting, just waiting. Doing nothing. It's unbearable,' she tailed off, hiccuped twice and devoured another fingernail. Mrs McLachlan silently refilled her employer's coffee cup.

Across the room, Latch tied a final knot in the rope binding the transformed Pronto. 'And *that*'ll put a bend in your chanter,' he muttered to his captive.

Signora Strega-Borgia wiped her nose on her

sleeve and began again. 'Titus? How long now? D'you think . . .'

'*MUM!*'

'Sorry. I just can't stand this . . .' she gulped another mouthful of coffee.

'Yes. You've told me. Ten times. Waiting. Just waiting. Doing nothing.'

'Titus, just because you *once* found me rolling around in a hot-toddy induced stupor, doesn't mean that you can treat me like an imbecile for the rest of time . . .'

Titus glared at his mother.

'It was a *mistake*, Titus. People make mistakes. Your father and I made a mistake when we split up. Mrs McLachlan made a mistake and turned that . . . that creature into a set of bagpipes . . .'

'Sab made a mistake,' added Latch helpfully.

Mrs McLachlan glared at him. Not *now*, she mouthed.

'Um er, no, he didn't,' amended Latch. '*I'm* mistaken.'

'I made a mistake,' admitted Titus. 'I sneezed my baby sister into the modem and sent her . . . sent her . . .' He burst into tears.

'Oh, Titus,' Signora Strega-Borgia wrapped her arms round her son's shaking shoulders. 'Oh, my dear, it was all a big mistake . . . what's *that*?'

'What?' sniffed Titus.

'On your computer television thingy,' she

flapped vaguely at the screen, 'YOU HAVE MAIL.'

'PANDORA!' yelled Titus. 'She's *BACK*!' His fingers flew over the keys, downloading the incoming mail and opening it as far as he could. 'Stand back,' he warned. 'Don't *breathe*.'

Signora Strega-Borgia sneezed carefully over her left shoulder. A large gobbet of goo flew across the room and landed on the fallen Pronto.

'Perfect,' said Latch with deep satisfaction.

'Oh *my*,' breathed Titus, backing away from the footstool on which the modem sat, 'Oh, *MY*.'

Appearing in front of him was an odd assortment of tiny shapes.

'Mum . . . it's *them*,' he said in an awed voice. 'They're back, but they're the wrong size. They're too *wee*.'

The tiny shapes waved and squeaked.

'Let me deal with this,' said Signora Strega-Borgia, producing a wand from her pocket. 'I'll soon have them back to life-size.' She began to mutter under her breath in Latin, passing her wand carefully over the heads of her miniaturized family. The tiny shapes grew bigger and bigger.

'Um . . . Mum, something's gone wrong,' said Titus in alarm. 'Remember what you were saying about mistakes?'

The tiny shapes were now life-size. Behind Titus, Mrs McLachlan buried her head in her hands. Signora Strega-Borgia's face turned an unhealthy shade of grey.

'Oh, *Pandora*,' said Titus sadly.

'*What?*' she yelled. 'What *now*?' She followed Titus's gaze downwards to where her feet should have been. 'Aaaargh! What are *those*?'

'Legs,' said Titus helpfully. 'Eight of them.'

'Oh NO,' wailed Pandora. 'Look at *Dad*!'

'What's wrong with me?' said Signor Strega-Borgia.

'Shall I tell him, or will you?' said Titus to his sister.

'Darling,' breathed Signora Strega-Borgia, 'your nether regions appear to have been confused with those of our littlest daughter . . .'

'My nether regions . . .' Signor Strega-Borgia repeated, looking down. 'Oh yeuuchh, excuse *me*, I need a nappy change.'

'And Dad, um . . . while you're about it,' said Titus, blushing deep crimson, 'you're wearing lipstick . . .'

'Somehow, I don't think I'm exactly cutting a dashing figure, what with a soggy bum and fuchsia-pink lips . . .'

'I don't care what you're wearing,' said Signora Strega-Borgia loyally. 'I'm just so glad to have you home.'

'Oh *baby*,' cooed Mrs McLachlan. 'My little . . . *no*, my *large* Damp . . . come to Nanny, pet.'

Blissfully unaware that she'd been transformed into an adult-sized infant, Damp stopped in mid-whimper and crawled towards her beloved nanny.

'Poor wee mite,' said Mrs McLachlan irrelevantly. 'Let's see if we can find you something to eat.'

'Better make that an adult portion,' suggested Titus, as the huge baby crawled slowly across the room.

'What about meEEEEE?' moaned Tarantella, crashing to the floor with a squawk. 'How you bipeds manage with only two legs, I cannot imagine.'

'Those are *my* legs,' Pandora said, in a voice that indicated they were only out on a temporary loan.

'And all eight of those fine furry ones that you're wearing are *mine*.'

'I'd better see if I can find some spells in one of my text books to undo this muddle,' said Signora Strega-Borgia.

'Later,' said her husband, wrapping his arms around her and their two older children. 'Magic can wait. Right now, we have all the magic we need . . .'

Amen to *that*, Mrs McLachlan silently avowed, leading the enormous Damp through the door and closing it behind her.

Husband and wife hugged each other long and hard, squeezing tight, not ever wanting to let go. Titus found his eyes watering alarmingly.

Latch hoisted the ex-Pronto onto his shoulders and coughed tactfully. 'Sir . . . Madam . . . shall I put this in the attic for now? I imagine we shan't be needing it for some time?'

'I'm determined to get the hang of this,' Tarantella muttered under her breath as, using the wall for support, she followed Latch out of the bedroom.

'Such an unflattering shade of pink,' said Signora Strega-Borgia, tenderly wiping lipstick off her husband's mouth.

I haven't seen her look this happy for . . . oh, *ages*, thought Pandora.

'Come on,' muttered Titus, pulling his sister out of the bedroom and closing the door behind him. 'They don't need us right now.'

'But, but . . . *I* need Mum,' wailed Pandora, waving a hairy leg for emphasis. 'She's the only one who can sort me out. Look, six surplus legs . . .'

'Later,' said Titus firmly, dragging her down the corridor. 'Meanwhile we have a few small matters to sort out.'

'Like what?' Pandora's voice came from the ceiling. 'Hey . . . being half spider, half human isn't all bad, you know. Look at MEEEEE.'

She scuttled along the cornice and with a nimble leap, hung upside down from a chandelier. Titus refused to be impressed.

'Like what happened to our wager?' he insisted. 'Remember? Tock? The ratlets?'

Pandora abruptly let herself down to the floor on a rope of spider silk. 'Suddenly,' she said, 'I've got an overwhelming desire for a nice crunchy bluebottle . . . or a sun-dried daddy-long-legs.'

'Stop trying to change the subject.'

'Titus, I can't swim the moat right now, can I? Think about it. Spiders *hate* water. All that Incy Wincy up the waterspout is nonsense. Show me a swimming spider and I'll show you a little bedraggled ball of ex-arachnid.'

'Absolutely,' agreed Tarantella, dropping into the conversation from the floor above. 'What are we talking about? Why does she have to swim the moat?'

Titus shuddered. As if his transformed sister wasn't bad enough, here was that revolting tarantula again. He took a deep breath and began, 'We had a bet. She had five days to find Multitudina's babies, or else she had to swim one lap of the moat.'

'*Them*,' spat Tarantella, 'those vile rodentettes? Those squeaky pink nastinesses. Well . . . that's *easy*. She has found them.'

'I have?' said Pandora.

'She *has*?' said Titus simultaneously.

'You *have*,' Tarantella said firmly. 'Think back. While we were enjoying the delights of exceeding the speed limit on the Web, we had a near collision. D'you recall? Coming towards us? Faster than a sneeze? Speed of light and all that stuff?'

Pandora's eyes grew wide. 'Oh that was *them*. I wondered why they seemed so familiar . . .'

Tarantella dangled from the ceiling, her twin legs tightly folded round her body. 'So let's have no more talk of moats,' she shivered, 'or spiders in baths,' she shuddered, 'and especially not that verminous baggage and her unspeakable offspring.'

'So I *did* find them,' said Pandora wonderingly. She felt ... oh, light, airy. Her body appeared to be filling up with millions of tiny bubbles. No bet, no moat, no CROCODILE! She extruded several feet of spider silk and launched herself off the banister into the lofty heights of the stairwell. 'FREEEEEEEeeeeee!' she yelled, as she vanished from sight.

Tarantella sighed. Still such a drama queen. Noise and theatrics. And, she decided, the girl has a lot to learn about spinning silk. She gazed at Titus. His mouth opened and shut and opened again.

'All I want to know is what happened to them? Where did they go?'

'I neither know, nor do I care,' said the spider. 'And now, if you'll excuse me, I'm going home.' Lurching inexpertly on her two new legs, Tarantella headed for her attic.

A Simple Twist of Fate

Professore Flense-Filleto removed his surgeon's gloves with an audible snap and dropped them in a pedal bin. Over the green theatre mask his eyes were red-rimmed with exhaustion. The operation had not been a success. In fact, due to a computer failure, it had been a disaster.

On the other side of the recovery room the anaesthetist frowned at his equipment and tapped it with a rubber-gloved finger. 'Useless machine,' he muttered, giving it a good kick. The heart monitor sprang to life, disgorging forty metres of graph paper from its chittering innards. 'That's better,' said the anaesthetist, scanning the printout. He patted a bandaged form lying on a trolley nearby. 'Thought you'd *died* on me for a minute . . .'

The nurse looked up from where she was counting blood-smeared scalpels onto a tray. 'When he wakes up, he'll probably wish he had.'

The Professore groaned and massaged the bridge of his nose. 'Thanks for the vote of confidence, Sister.'

The hospital cleaner stopped disinfecting the floor and languidly rinsed his mop in a rusted steel bucket. Pink-tinged water slopped out over its side. 'What a *massacre*,' he moaned, 'blood everywhere . . . d'you have to be so sloppy? This job's taking me twice as long as usual, and I'm still not done yet . . .'

'All right, ALL RIGHT!' yelled the Professore. '*So*. I make a mistake, huh? We all make mistakes. Nobody is perfect. My father rest his soul always said to me as he filleted the pork bellies and the lamb shanks and the ox hearts, in this life, sonny, nobody's perfect . . . not even your mamma.'

'Hey, come on,' said the anaesthetist, 'lighten up. It's hardly your fault, Professore. So, there was a major fault with the computer link-up, right?' Despite the silence that greeted this question, he warmed to his theme. 'So, there's a bunch of nomadic rodents on the Net, right? And they get mixed up in the computer-generated model we're working from to remodel this guy's face, right? Not your fault. So, this guy wakes up, right?' He prodded the silent body on the trolley. 'He looks in the mirror and he goes 'WHAT'S *THIS*?' and he sues you, right? You sue the computer company,

198 ____

right? The computer company sues its supplier of microprocessors . . .'

'Right?' interrupted the Professore, catching on at last.

'The supplier of microprocessors fires a worker on its assembly line,' the anaesthetist paused for effect.

'RIGHT!' chorused the nurse and the cleaner.

'And . . .' the anaesthetist added, 'the worker on the assembly line goes home and yells at the wife and kids . . .'

'He's coming round,' warned the nurse.

Don di S'Embowelli was swimming in a blood-filled fish tank. Suspended, drifting in claustrophobic redness around him were the skeletons of the hapless Ragu plus countless other bodies whose lives the Don had taken. He thrashed and gargled, trying to reach the surface . . . the light . . . the air . . . Squeaking pitifully, he exploded into daylight . . . into an echoing steel hell with his senses magnified a hundredfold. The smell of disinfectant burned his bandaged nose, the light seared his bandaged eyes and every noise crashed and boomed like thunder in his ears.

Nearby came an oceanic splashing followed by a rhythmic swish swish, then a voice grated in his ear, 'F' I was you, Signor, I'd sue them for every-thing . . .'

'Squeak, eek, squee?' said the Don.

'Feeling better, Signor?' This new voice was

accompanied by a deluge of cheap perfume. 'Don't try to say anything just yet.'

'Squeee! SQUEAK, EEE, *eek*!' said the Don.

'Bad luck, old chap,' said a third voice, growing painfully loud as its owner approached where the Don lay. 'We ran into some little problems during your operation, but nothing that we can't sort out with two years of intensive corrective surgery . . .'

'Eek, EEEK SQUEEE,' shrieked the Don, thrashing his bandaged head from side to side.

'NURSE!' yelled the aneasthetist. 'Hold his head, I'm going to put him under again.'

The Don's plaintive squeakings grew fainter as he slipped back underneath the red tide again, his new whiskers streaming behind him. Swimming, he decided, was easier when you used your pink tail as a rudder.

Sorted

'**R**ight,' said Signora Strega-Borgia, with a confidence that she didn't feel. 'Let's get this muddle sorted out.'

The family were gathered in the library at StregaSchloss, smiling for the camera as Pandora took a photograph of them all. 'Just one last one, Mum, but with me in it,' she said, passing the camera to her mother and scuttling across the floor and up the wall to dangle upside down from the cornice.

Tarantella crossed and re-crossed her human legs and rolled her eyes. 'Oh come *on*,' she demanded peevishly, 'I was halfway through the most *delicious* dinner when you dragged me back down here.'

'SMILE,' said Signora Strega-Borgia. They smiled and the camera captured the moment for ever:

Signor Strega-Borgia standing, one arm on the mantelpiece, clad in a dry nappy, Tarantella gazing into the camera with her legs draped over the arm of a chair, Damp asleep propped up against a pinnacle of books, Titus in his pyjamas affecting total boredom as Pandora swung back and forth in front of him, suspended on a lumpy length of spider-silk . . .

'Did it flash?' wondered Signora Strega-Borgia to herself, peering into the lens of the camera, before laying it down on a nearby chair.

The mantelpiece clock began to chime midnight.

'Now . . . um, let's see if I can understand this.' Signora Strega-Borgia leafed through an enormous leather-bound book, chewing the end of her wand thoughtfully.

The family waited. Impatiently, Signor Strega-Borgia demanded, 'Darling are you *sure* you're going to get it right this time? What if you turn us all into cockroaches or worse?'

Signora Strega-Borgia threw her wand to the floor and burst into tears.

The library door opened to reveal Mrs McLachlan bearing a laden tray. 'Now, dear,' she said, ignoring the loud sobs coming from her employer, 'what we all need is a good strong cup of tea and maybe a wee fruit scone, or perhaps some of my seed cake, or fudge cake, or lemon drench cake, or plum cake or banana loaf, or maybe,' she paused, ascertained that the Signora was still weeping, '. . . or maybe you're not hungry?'

She placed the tea tray firmly on top of the open book of spells, and picked up the discarded wand. 'Such a nuisance, these things,' she declared. 'Simply not up to the job.' Signora Strega-Borgia looked up, her tear-stained face showing a faint glimmer of hope. 'Now, dear,' continued Mrs McLachlan, cutting the fudge cake into several generous wedges, 'I've washed and ironed your best wand, and it's waiting for you on the kitchen table. Why don't you pop downstairs and get it, and meanwhile I'll pour you a cup of tea?'

Obediently, Signora Strega-Borgia headed downstairs to the kitchen. As soon as the sound of her footsteps faded away, Mrs McLachlan pulled a small perspex box from her pocket and fixed the family with a basilisk-like glare. 'Not one *word*,' she commanded, holding up her hand for silence. 'Not one word now, and not a squeak when the Signora returns, or there'll be no cake. One day the Signora might become a very fine witch, but she'll never do it unless she *thinks* she can.' Flipping open her make-up box, Mrs McLachlan began to type.

Mrs McLachlan met Signora Strega-Borgia clutching her laundered wand in the corridor outside the library. 'Not that I know the first thing about magic, dear, but . . . might I make a wee suggestion?' Signora Strega-Borgia bit her bottom lip and nodded. 'I've turned out the lights in the Library to aid your concentration. There's just enough light coming from the fireplace to allow you to see where to point your nice clean wand. Maybe you were just distracted last time by the sight of your loved ones in such a pickle? So ... my advice, for what it's worth, is do *not* turn the lights back on until you're finished. That way you won't be able to see their wee faces, and you'll be able to concentrate on doing your Magic.' Patting Signora Strega-Borgia on the arm, Mrs McLachlan opened the Library door and led her employer inside.

In the flickering firelight, Signora Strega-Borgia could just about make out the shapes of her family huddled by the fireplace. A thin and hairy leg waved encouragingly in her direction, followed by a hissed, 'Tarantella ... PAN, I mean, don't distract her!'

A stifled sob from Damp firmed up Signora Strega-Borgia's resolve. I *won't* fail, she decided, I simply *can't*. My family needs me. I CAN do this. I think I am a good enough witch. She amended the last bit, I AM a good enough witch. I am. I am. Slowly, holding her breath, fingers tightly crossed, she began to spin. Behind her, holding Pandora's camera, Mrs McLachlan waited.

Just as Signora Strega-Borgia stopped in mid-spin and pointed her trembling wand at her family, Mrs McLachlan pressed the shutter release on the camera. It flashed, Signora Strega-Borgia gasped and rushed to turn on the lights.

'Oh well *done*, dear,' said Mrs McLachlan, prompting the family with a glare.

'Um ... er ... well DONE, Mum,' said Titus, catching on.

'What a star,' added Tarantella, clapping all eight legs.

'How ever *did* you do that?' said Signor Strega-Borgia and Pandora in perfect stereo.

'Oh ...' said Signora Strega-Borgia, casually stirring her teacup with her wand, 'it was easy.'

At least, noted Mrs McLachlan, carrying Damp upstairs to bed, she had the grace to blush ...

The Taste of Summer

'**O**h, Marie, you shouldn't have!' cried Mrs McLachlan. 'A cake! For my birthday! How *kind*.' She hugged the blushing cook and gazed at the cake in disbelief.

'What an *unusual* colour,' murmured Signora Strega-Borgia, 'I've always thought grey so stylish . . . come on, Ffup, do the candles, pet.'

The dragon obligingly leaned forward and squirted flames from each nostril. Immediately the entire cake was alight.

'*Fifty* candles,' whispered Titus, 'Eughh. I don't ever want to be *that* old.'

'That can be arranged,' Pandora replied.

Mrs McLachlan took a huge breath.

'Make a wish, make a wish,' Pandora pleaded.

Mrs McLachlan winked, and exhaled.

'Bravo!' cheered Signor Strega-Borgia, lifting his glass to her. 'Now your wish will come true.'

'But you *can't* tell us what it was,' Pandora said hopefully.

'But you *can* cut the cake,' said Signora Strega-Borgia.

Marie Bain handed Mrs McLachlan a knife and scuttled back to the kitchen for plates.

It had been a perfect day, thought Titus. If it had been *my* birthday wish, he decided, I would have wished that every day could be just like this one. Following a morning of unbroken sunshine, they had eaten lunch in the garden and now, replete and sleepy with happiness, the family and assorted pets lounged on the lawn on blankets and deckchairs, watching the sun slide into the sea loch. Late afternoon sunshine painted StregaSchloss gold, gilded them all in its gentle light and drove the scent of honeysuckle out into the still air.

If it had been *my* birthday wish, thought Pandora as she watched Mrs McLachlan struggle to cut through the grey icing, I'd have wished for a different cake . . .

A shadow fell across the tablecloth. 'Nonna!' Signora Strega-Borgia struggled to her feet. 'What a pleasant surprise!'

'And you thought *fifty* was old . . .' Pandora whispered to her brother.

A very wrinkly old lady was dripping over the remains of lunch. 'Someone defrosted me . . .' she

mumbled, then caught sight of the cake. 'How kind
. . . A cake . . . For me? Is it my birthday? Again?'

'Welcome back, Nonna.' Signora Strega-Borgia
led the old woman to a deckchair and gently folded
her into it. 'Some tea? Champagne? Strawberries?'

'Have they found it yet?' the old woman asked.
Her voice sounded painfully dry, like the rustle of
papery leaves, words made of dust. 'The *cure*, you
know,' she added. 'You *do* remember, don't you?'
Her watery eyes fixed pleadingly on Signora
Strega-Borgia.

'No, Nonna,' she said. 'Not yet.'

Strega-Nonna shrank into her deckchair. In the
sunshine, her skin was almost transparent. At her
feet, Sab slumped with a small grunt. The old lady
smiled, causing her face to crease up like a walnut.
Creaking slightly, she bent forward to pat the
gryphon's leathery head. 'Dear faithful beast,' she
murmured, 'you're wearing your six hundred years
better than I am . . .' The gryphon looked up at her
in adoration. 'I miss our conversations,' she mused,
'our long walks . . . That freezer is pretty lonely, I
can tell you. Still . . . one day . . .'

Two large tears squeezed out from under the
gryphon's eyelids.

Strega-Nonna levered herself to her feet.
Painfully she bent down and took a strawberry
from the fruit bowl. Titus watched, fascinated, as
she popped it into her gummy mouth, mumbled it
around for a moment and swallowed. 'Summer . . .'

she said, hobbling back to the house. 'The taste of all those summers . . .' She vanished into the shadowy doorway of StregaSchloss. Sab gave a small whimper.

'What did she mean, "a cure"?' said Pandora.

'For old age, sweetheart,' sniffed Signora Strega-Borgia, dabbing at her eyes with her napkin. 'She's waiting till they find a cure for old age, then she'll stop living in the freezer.'

'But can't you cure her?' said Titus. 'You know, with a spell or something? Magic her back to being young?'

Signora Strega-Borgia sighed. 'There are some things, Titus, that are way beyond my limited magical powers. A cure for old age is one of them.'

The group on the lawn were silent as they considered this. A tortoiseshell butterfly alighted on the cake, sampled some of the grey icing and keeled over with a dying beat of its wings.

'Poor Nonna,' said Pandora. 'It must be awful just lying there with only ice cream and fish fingers for company.'

'It's her choice,' said Signor Strega-Borgia. 'But personally, I think she's making a big mistake . . .'

'It's a family failing.' Signora Strega-Borgia smiled at Titus. 'Don't worry, she really is quite happy in her own way. Every time we have a power cut she re-appears, says hello, asks if there have been any advances in science and then goes back to sleep. She's been doing it for *centuries*.'

'What did she do before freezers were invented?' asked Titus.

'She lived near the North Pole,' said his mother, 'in an iceberg. Under the Aurora with whales and polar bears for company, not to mention millions of cod.'

'I have the plates, Meeesus McCacclong,' called Marie Bain, emerging from the shadows round the house. She squinted in the sunlight, twisting her hands in her apron.

'Oh *Lord*,' said Mrs McLachlan, reminded of the cake. She renewed her efforts with the knife, but the icing remained immune to her assaults.

'What *is* this stuff?' she demanded as the knife tip snapped off and pinged into a leftover bowl of potato salad. 'Concrete?'

'Yes,' said the cook, blissfully unaware of the effect this admission had on the assembled company. 'Ees Readymix Concrete, eet say zo on ze packet.'

'Marie, dear,' said Mrs McLachlan, 'could you be an angel and bring me another knife? This one seems to be broken.'

As the cook disappeared kitchenwards once more, Mrs McLachlan removed a small box from her pocket.

Latch signed – there she goes again, he thought, vanity, vanity . . .

There was a bright flash accompanied by the smell of burning sugar.

'Heavens!' Signora Strega-Borgia said admiringly, displaying an abysmal ignorance of all things culinary. 'How did you do *that*? Is it like a blowtorch? A sort of portable-microwave thingy? What a clever thing.'

Latch stared at Mrs McLachlan. He put two and two together and arrived at pi r squared.

'*This* time,' she said to him under her breath, 'I didn't miss my target.'

She raised her voice to its normal volume and added, 'Marie – the knife, how very kind, dear. Now . . . cake, everyone?'

Swimming with the Crocodile

The first stars were appearing in the sky as the family finished Mrs McLachlan's birthday lunch. The cake had been devoured down to the last smear of icing and Knot lay under a chestnut tree, slowly chewing his way through his forty-third pink candle.

Latch and Mrs McLachlan shook the tablecloth free of crumbs, the antique linen weave catching the last of the evening light. For an instant they were joined by this luminous cloth as they folded and refolded it into a neat parcel.

Signor and Signora Strega-Borgia ambled down to the lochside to watch the sun leach out into the sea. Titus noted with some satisfaction that they had their arms wrapped tightly around each other.

'I think they're going to be all right, Titus,' said

Pandora. 'We can stop worrying about them.'

'Eugh, they're *kissing*,' groaned Titus, his delighted expression betraying how happy he was to see his parents engaging in such revolting behaviour.

Pandora sighed and rolled over onto her stomach. 'I've eaten too much,' she remarked happily.

'Pig,' said Titus.

Pandora ignored him, reaching out to scoop left-over chicken legs and salami sandwiches into a bowl.

Titus watched her with horror. 'You're not . . .' he said.

'Eat this lot?' she balanced the bowl on top of a tureen full of potato salad. 'Don't be ridiculous, I'm going to feed Tock. Keep me company?'

'I'll come in a minute,' Titus yawned and stretched crabwise in the dewy grass. He watched his sister disappear round the side of StregaSchloss, heading for the moat. After a whole day of sun and food he felt too full to move, just yet. Overhead, the familiar constellations winked into being, pinpricked against a lilac sky. Bats flew out from the eaves of the house, skilfully avoiding the treetops in their nocturnal quest for food.

The water in the moat was still, mirroring the moon rising over the distant hills. Pandora placed her offerings on the warm stone that rimmed Tock's home, and sat down to wait. On the far bank, a frantic thrashing amongst the waterlilies indicated that she wouldn't have to linger long.

With a series of rusty creaks and honks, Tock's snout broke water a metre away from Pandora. Ancient yellow eyes met her green ones. Pandora shivered. The sight of all those teeth, askew like tombstones in a disused graveyard, reminded her of her recent narrow escape. Tock's nostrils flared as he caught wind of his dinner. He sped towards it, throwing up a wave in his wake. Pandora leapt to her feet and jumped backwards, just as the crocodile hurled itself out of the water.

Much to Pandora's relief, she was not the reason for Tock's haste. The crocodile ignored her completely, burying his nose in the pile of salami sandwiches. Greedily, he opened his jaws wide, and then appeared to undergo a change of heart. After devouring two of Pronto's henchmen plus their knife and machine-gun, the crocodile had taken a vow never to touch flesh again, especially not of the weapon-bearing kind.

'Blark,' he honked, pointing to the salami. 'Glurk ploot phitui.'

'I beg your pardon?' Pandora said, not understanding one word.

'Glop. Splug ... drekk,' explained Tock, de-salami-ing the sandwiches and tossing the discarded pink circles into the undergrowth.

'You don't like salami?' Pandora enquired.

'Drekk yrrg. Meat-blah,' Tock said, investigating the contents of the tureen.

'You're a recent convert to vegetarianism?' Pandora said, astonished. In her mind a wild plan began to take shape.

'Gaw titin wun,' Tock said, wolfing potato salad. On reflection, he picked up the tureen and ate it as well. Displaying alarming amounts of teeth in a grin, he waddled back into the moat and glided effortlessly away into the darkness just as Titus came looking for his sister.

To Titus's horror, he arrived in time to see Pandora strip down to her underwear and dip a foot in the water of the moat. She's *not*, he thought, breaking into a run.

Without turning her head to show that she'd spotted him, Pandora said, 'So. I'm a wuss, am I? A scaredy sissy? A cowardy cuss?'

'Pan. Don't do it. The bet's off.'

'Maybe so,' she said, straightening her arms out in front of her, 'but you'll always think that I ratted on the deal.'

'No. Well . . . maybe,' admitted Titus.

Pandora rose on her toes and brought her arms together over her head. On the far side of the moat, in an area of deepest shade, something stirred. Something that hadn't eaten a nanny for weeks.

'Please, Pandora – DON'T DO THIS,' Titus begged, reaching the moatside at exactly the same time as his sister dived into the water. Large waves splashed over the stone surround, soaking Titus's feet. From the area of deepest darkness a wave of displaced water arrowed towards Pandora's point of entry. 'OH NO . . .' Titus was terrified.

This was worse than sending your baby sibling down the Internet, far worse than finding your mother drunk, worse even than being held at gunpoint . . . he simply couldn't imagine life without Pandora. As he flung himself into the moat, Titus remembered that for him, swimming lessons had been a complete wash-out. WHAT AM I DOING? he panicked, water closing over his head. I CAN'T EVEN SWIM AND THERE'S A RAVENING REPTILE IN HERE SOMEWHERE . . .

'HELP!' he screamed, surfacing. 'HELP! HELP! I'M DROWNING!'

'Don't be such a wuss,' said a familiar voice.

I'm dead, thought Titus, I'm hearing things. An unstoppable force propelled him at speed across the moat. Titus opened his eyes. He was pinioned across Tock's snout. 'NO!' he shrieked. 'HELP! I'M BEING EATEN BY A CROCODILE! SAVE ME!'

In exasperation the crocodile's slitty eyes rolled backwards in its head. With an effortless jerk of his neck muscles, Tock tossed Titus onto his scaly back and set off across the moat again.

Suddenly remembering why he'd jumped into the moat in the first place, Titus wrapped his arms around Tock's neck and tried to throttle his sister's assassin.

'Aaah,' said Tock. No-one had ever hugged him before. To show his appreciation, he playfully nibbled Titus's arms.

'AAUGHH. HE'S GOT ME! I'M DYING!'

'Titus, for heaven's sake, do shut up.'

'Pandora? You're *alive*?'

'Yes. And so are you,' Pandora said, treading water in front of him. 'Tock, let *go* of him.'

The crocodile released his grip on Titus's arms.

To Titus's embarrassment, they weren't even scratched.

'Titus, what are you doing in the moat?'

'Rescuing you from this beast.'

'Oh Titus . . . what a *brave* thing to do.'

'No,' Titus said, edging warily along Tock's back, away from the rows of teeth, 'it wasn't brave it was stu . . .'

His words were lost in an explosion of bubbles as Tock dived underwater. Titus found himself gripped in a strong pair of arms and towed back to the surface again.

'Pandora,' he spluttered, half-drowned. 'What are you doing?'

'Rescuing *you*, brother mine.' She expertly struck out for dry land, cupping Titus's chin in her hand. 'Rescuing you from yourself . . .'

'Why didn't you tell me?' Latch moaned. 'Instead of letting me make an idiot of myself . . .'

Mrs McLachlan gazed up at the night sky where

the wheeling shapes of Sab and Ffup were silhouetted against the stars. 'You didn't make an idiot of yourself, dear. On the contrary, you were exceedingly brave.'

'But that box of yours,' insisted Latch. 'You should have said . . .'

Mrs McLachlan dropped her gaze to meet his. 'Said *what*?' she demanded. ' "O Latch, here I have a wee box that combines a super-intelligent computer with some good old-fashioned magic, so step back and let little old me take care of this gun-wielding criminal . . ." or, "Move over, dear and let a real witch take care of this." Get real, laddie – you'd never have believed me.'

'Um.' Latch scratched furiously under his kilt. 'Er . . . yes . . . you're absolutely right. But I believe you *now*.' He paused and suddenly pleaded, 'Flora – could you use it, the box, to do something about this stupid tartan skirt?'

Mrs McLachlan's laughter rang out over the meadow, merging with the distant putter of the night-time lobster boat that tracked a line of silver across the sea loch.

In the Schloss kitchen, Marie Bain dozed in an ancient settle, her slipperless feet propped on Knot's woolly back, a cookery book open spine-up across her lap.

In the pantry the mended freezer hummed and clicked, drawing Strega-Nonna deeper and deeper into permafrost.

* * *

'Titus,' said Pandora, appearing at his bedroom door.

'Nhuh?' He looked up from the pages of a computer manual.

'Can I come in? My bedroom's a tip, I've got nothing to read and I've only got a pile of broken matchsticks to sleep on.'

'You think *you've* got problems,' Titus said, flicking through his manual. 'My CD-ROM's broken. I took it apart and found *some*one had stuffed bacon rinds in it.'

'Yeuuchhh,' said Pandora. 'That sounds like the kind of stunt that Damp would pull . . .'

'Babies are so gross,' said Titus.

'I'm *never* going to have any when I'm old,' said Pandora.

'I'm *never* going to grow old,' vowed Titus. '*Fifty* candles!'

'Six *hundred* candles,' groaned Pandora.

'You'd never be able to blow them out,' said Titus.

'Want a bet?' said Pandora.

'*NO*,' said Titus.

Damp stretched like a small starfish. Her parents on either side of her groaned and clung onto their tiny allowance of edge-of-bed. The baby lay in the darkness, surrounded by the smell of sleep that clung to the eiderdown, debating whether to whimper, grizzle or go back to sleep. Something had woken her up. Her eyes flicked open. There it was again – a scratching noise. She couldn't see anything, even with the full moon shining across the bedroom and pooling on the floor over by the fireplace. Damp's eyelids closed slowly, her eyelashes casting long shadows across her cheeks. Her mothlike breath changed to something heavier, and within moments she was deeply asleep.

Under the bed, Multitudina groaned and clutched her distended stomach with both front paws. Never, never, never again, she vowed. Too much like hard work, she reminded herself in between groans. And besides, she thought frivolously, I'll *never* get my girlish figure back if I keep on having babies. Two minutes later, she was gazing in surprise at a tiny pink replica of herself. Was that it? she wondered, just the *one*? Phew, got off lightly then – here was me expecting to be expecting at least six . . . The tiny bald ratlet opened its mouth to demand room service. As for your name, Multitudina thought, expertly tucking her daughter under one arm, I've decided to call you Terminus . . .

THE END

ABOUT THE AUTHOR

Debi Gliori is the highly successful author and illustrator of more than forty picture books for children. She is best known for her *Mr Bear* series, which has sold over 1.5 million copies worldwide in territories from Japan to America, and for her collaborations with Joyce Dunbar on *Tell Me Something Happy Before I Go to Sleep* and *Tell Me What It's Like to Be Big*.

Pure Dead Magic is Debi Gliori's first novel, and the start of a wonderful trilogy about the Strega-Borgia family. Debi says she was inspired to make her first foray into longer fiction by the approach of her fortieth birthday and a desire to prove to those ignorant people who kep asking her when she was going to write a 'proper' book that she could do it.

Debi was born in Glasgow and trained at Edinburgh College of Art, at the end of which she received a travelling scholarship and went to Milan to soak up Italian design. Since then Debi has freelanced as an illustrator, initially in advertising, and for the last 12 years working exclusively in publishing. She now lives near Edinburgh and, at weekends, on the west coast of Scotland.

Pure Dead Magic was largely written while curled up on the sofa, after Debi's five children were in bed. Now, however, Debi has a purpose-built studio in her back garden where she can usually write, paint or think in peace.

In the tiny amounts of spare time that she can claw back from a rather crammed life, she loves cooking and gardening, but she's always tended to look a tad embarrassed if asked what her hobbies are, 'since I don't appear to have any . . .'

PURE DEAD WICKED
Debi Gliori

Disaster strikes at StregaSchloss!

The roof of the old castle is falling down and
the Strega-Borgia family have to move out.
The mythical beasts and the magical nanny
come too. But the talking tarantula, the frozen
granny and a trickle of tincture are left
behind . . .

The hilarious sequel to *Pure Dead Magic*,
now available in Doubleday hardback

0 552 54847 2

CORGI BOOKS

ALL THE KING'S HORSES
Laura C. Stevenson

It began the day Grandpa escaped . . .

Something very odd has happened to Colin and Sarah's much-loved grandfather. It's as if a stranger is inhabitating his body . . . as if Grandpa has been spirited away and a changeling left in his place. Raised all their lives on his tales of great heroes and fantastical legendary creatures, Colin and Sarah feel sure that the Faer Folk are involved.

In an attempt to find him again, they follow Grandpa's path, crossing the boundary between the everyday world and the enchantments of the Otherworld . . .

A wonderfully lyrical fantasy adventure brimming with characters from the Otherworld – from magnificent horses to mischievous night-elves and the legendary Sidhe.

0 552 54718 2

A CORGI ORIGINAL PAPERBACK

BEYOND THE DEEPWOODS –
THE EDGE CHRONICLES
Paul Stewart and Chris Riddell

"Your destiny lies beyond the Deepwoods . . ."

Abandoned at birth in the perilous Deepwoods, Twig is brought up by a family of woodtrolls. One cold night, Twig does what no woodtroll has ever done before – *he strays from the path.*

So begins a heart-stopping adventure that will take Twig through a nightmare world of goblins and trogs, bloodthirsty beasts and flesh-eating trees. One desire alone drives Twig on: the longing to discover his true identity and his destiny . . .

Created by an exciting new writing team, this compelling fantasy, with its brilliantly witty illustrations, is set to become a future classic.

'At the sharp end of today's fantasy novels . . .'
The Times

'Fabulously illustrated . . . and written with more than usual elegance'
Sunday Times

'A richly inventive fantasy'
Literary Review

0 552 54592 9

CORGI BOOKS